Margaret Atwood

was born in Ottawa in 1939. She spent much of her early life in northern Ontario and Quebec. She is Canada's most eminent novelist, poet and critic. Her first volume of poetry, *The Circle Game* (1966), won the Governor-General's Award. Since then she has published nine novels, five collections of short fiction and fourteen volumes of poetry. Her first novel, *The Edible Woman*, was published in 1969 and was followed by *Surfacing, Lady Oracle, Life Before Man, Bodily Harm, The Handmaid's Tale* – Winner of the Arthur C. Clarke Award for Science Fiction and the Governor-General's Award, and now a major film – *Cat's Eye, The Robber Bride* and *Alias Grace*, winner of the Canadian Giller Prize in 1996. Her most recent three novels have all been also shortlisted for the Booker Prize. *Eating Fire: Selected Poetry 1965–1995* contains three previously published collections: *Poems: 1965–1975, Poems 1976–1986* and *Morning in the Burned House* (1995). Margaret Atwood lives in Toronto with the writer Graeme Gibson and their daughter.

Also by Margaret Atwood

Novels

The Edible Woman
Surfacing
Lady Oracle
Life Before Man
Bodily Harm
The Handmaid's Tale
Cat's Eye
The Robber Bride
Alias Grace

Short Stories

Dancing Girls
Bluebeard's Egg
Wilderness Tips

Short Fictions

Good Bones
Murder in the Dark
Bones and Murder

Poetry
Selected Poems 1965–1975
Selected Poems 1976–1986
Morning in the Burned House

SURFACING

Margaret Atwood

A *Virago* Book

Published by Virago Press 1979

Reprinted 1982, 1983, 1984, 1985, 1987, 1988, 1989,
1990, 1991, 1994 (twice), 1995, 1996, 1997, 1998, 1999

First published in Great Britain by
André Deutsch Ltd and Wildwood House 1972

A CIP catalogue record for this book is
available from the British Library.

ISBN 0 86068 064 9

Printed and bound in Great Britain by Clays Ltd, St Ives plc

Virago
A Division of
Little, Brown and Company (UK)
Brettenham House
Lancaster Place
London WC2E 7EN

ONE

Chapter One

I can't believe I'm on this road again, twisting along past the lake where the white birches are dying, the disease is spreading up from the south, and I notice they now have sea-planes for hire. But this is still near the city limits; we didn't go through, it's swelled enough to have a bypass, that's success.

I never thought of it as a city but as the last or first outpost depending on which way we were going, an accumulation of sheds and boxes and one main street with a movie theatre, the itz, the oyal, red R burnt out, and two restaurants which served identical grey hamburger steaks plastered with mud gravy and canned peas, watery and pallid as fisheyes, and french fries bleary with lard. Order a poached egg, my mother said, you can tell if it's fresh by the edges.

In one of those restaurants before I was born my brother got under the table and slid his hands up and down the waitress's legs while she was bringing the food; it was during the war and she had on shiny orange rayon stockings, he'd never seen them before, my mother didn't wear them. A different year there we ran through the snow across the sidewalk in our bare feet because we had no shoes, they'd worn out during the summer. In the car that time we sat with our feet wrapped in blankets, pretending we were wounded. My brother said the Germans shot our feet off.

Now though I'm in another car, David's and Anna's; it's sharp-finned and striped with chrome, a lumbering monster left over from ten years ago, he has to reach under the instrument panel to turn on the lights. David says they can't afford a newer one, which probably isn't true. He's a good driver, I realize that, I keep my outside hand on the door in spite of it. To brace myself and so I can get out quickly if I have to. I've driven in the same car with them before but on this road it doesn't seem right, either the three of them are in the wrong place or I am.

I'm in the back seat with the packsacks; this one, Joe, is sitting beside me chewing gum and holding my hand, they both pass the time. I examine the hand: the palm is broad, the short fingers tighten and relax, fiddling with my gold ring, turning it, it's a reflex of his. He has peasant hands, I have peasant feet, Anna told us that. Everyone now can do a little magic, she reads hands at parties, she says it's a substitute for conversation. When she did mine she said "Do you have a twin?" I said No. "Are you positive," she said, "because some of your lines are double." Her index finger traced me: "You had a good childhood but then there's this funny break." She puckered her forehead and I said I just wanted to know how long I was going to live, she could skip the rest. After that she told us Joe's hands were dependable but not sensitive and I laughed, which was a mistake.

From the side he's like the buffalo on the u.s. nickel, shaggy and blunt-snouted, with small clenched eyes and the defiant but insane look of a species once dominant, now threatened with extinction. That's how he thinks of himself too: deposed, unjustly. Secretly he would like them to set up a kind of park for him, like a bird sanctuary. Beautiful Joe.

He feels me watching him and lets go of my hand. Then he takes his gum out, bundling it in the silver wrapper, and sticks it in the ashtray and crosses his arms. That means I'm not supposed to observe him; I face front.

In the first few hours of driving we moved through flattened cow-sprinkled hills and leaf trees and dead elm skeletons, then into the needle trees and the cuttings dynamited in pink and grey granite and the flimsy tourist cabins, and the signs saying GATEWAY TO THE NORTH, at least four towns claim to be that. The future is in the North, that was a political slogan once; when my father heard it he said there was nothing in the North but the past and not much of that either. Wherever he is now, dead or alive and nobody knows which, he's no longer making epigrams. They have no right to get old. I envy people whose parents died when they were young, that's easier to remember, they stay unchanged. I was sure mine would anyway, I could leave and return much later and everything would be the same. I thought of them as living in some other time, going about their own concerns closed safe behind a wall as translucent as jello, mammoths frozen in a glacier. All I would have to do was come back when I was ready but I kept putting it off, there would be too many explanations.

Now we're passing the turnoff to the pit the Americans hollowed out. From here it looks like an innocent hill, spruce-covered, but the thick power lines running into the forest give it away. I heard they'd left, maybe that was a ruse, they could easily still be living in there, the generals in concrete bunkers and the ordinary soldiers in underground apartment buildings where the lights burn all the time. There's no way of checking because we aren't allowed in. The city invited them to stay, they were good for business, they drank a lot.

"That's where the rockets are," I say. *Were*. I don't correct it.

David says "Bloody fascist pig Yanks," as though he's commenting on the weather.

Anna says nothing. Her head rests on the back of the seat, the ends of her light hair whipping in the draft from the side window that won't close properly. Earlier she was singing, House of the Rising Sun and Lili Marlene, both of them several times, trying to make her voice go throaty and deep; but it came out like a hoarse child's. David turned on the radio, he couldn't get anything, we were between stations. When she was in the middle of St. Louis Blues he began to whistle and she stopped. She's my best friend, my best woman friend; I've known her two months.

I lean forward and say to David, "The bottle house is around this next curve and to the left," and he nods and slows the car. I told them about it earlier, I guessed it was the kind of object that would interest them. They're making a movie, Joe is doing the camera work, he's never done it before but David says they're the new Renaissance Men, you teach yourself what you need to learn. It was mostly David's idea, he calls himself the director: they already have the credits worked out. He wants to get shots of things they come across, random samples he calls them, and that will be the name of the movie too: *Random Samples*. When they've used up their supply of film (which was all they could afford; and the camera is rented) they're going to look at what they've collected and rearrange it.

"How can you tell what to put in if you don't already know what it's about?" I asked David when he was describing it. He gave me one of his initiate-to-novice stares. "If you close your mind in advance like that you wreck it. What you need is flow." Anna, over by the stove measuring out the coffee, said everyone she knew was making a movie, and David said that was no fucking reason why he shouldn't. She said "You're right, sorry"; but she laughs about it behind his back, she calls it Random Pimples.

The bottle house is built of pop bottles cemented together with the bottoms facing out, green ones and brown ones in zig-zag patterns like the ones they taught us in school to draw on teepees; there's a wall around it made of bottles too, arranged in letters so the brown ones spell BOTTLE VILLA.

"Neat," David says, and they get out of the car with the camera. Anna and I climb out after them; we stretch our arms, and Anna has a cigarette. She's wearing a purple tunic and white bellbottoms, they have a smear on them already, grease

4

from the car. I told her she should wear jeans or something but she said she looks fat in them.

"Who made it, Christ, think of the work," she says, but I don't know anything about it except that it's been there forever, the tangled black spruce swamp around it making it even more unlikely, a preposterous monument to some quirkish person exiled or perhaps a voluntary recluse like my father, choosing this swamp because it was the only place where he could fulfill his lifelong dream of living in a house of bottles. Inside the wall is an attempted lawn and a border with orange mattress-tuft marigolds.

"Great," says David, "really neat," and he puts his arm around Anna and hugs her briefly to show he's pleased, as though she is somehow responsible for the Bottle Villa herself. We get back in the car.

I watch the side windows as though it's a T.V. screen. There's nothing I can remember till we reach the border, marked by the sign that says BIENVENUE on one side and WELCOME on the other. The sign has bullet holes in it, rusting red around the edges. It always did, in the fall the hunters use it for target practice; no matter how many times they replace it or paint it the bullet holes reappear, as though they aren't put there but grow by a kind of inner logic or infection, like mould or boils. Joe wants to film the sign but David says "Naaa, what for?"

Now we're on my home ground, foreign territory. My throat constricts, as it learned to do when I discovered people could say words that would go into my ears meaning nothing. To be deaf and dumb would be easier. The cards they poke at you when they want a quarter, with the hand alphabet on them. Even so, you would need to learn spelling.

The first smell is the mill, sawdust, there are mounds of it in the yard with the stacked timber slabs. The pulpwood goes elsewhere to the paper mill, but the bigger logs are corralled in a boom on the river, a ring of logs chained together with the free ones nudging each other inside it; they travel to the saws in a clanking overhead chute, that hasn't been changed. The car goes under it and we're curving up into the tiny company town, neatly planned with public flowerbeds and an eighteenth century fountain in the middle, stone dolphins and a cherub with part of the face missing. It looks like an imitation but it may be real.

Anna says "Oh wow, what a great fountain."

"The company built the whole thing," I say, and David says "Rotten capitalist bastards" and begins to whistle again.

I tell him to turn right and he does. The road ought to be here, but instead there's a battered chequerboard, the way is blocked.

"Now what," says David.

We didn't bring a map because I knew we wouldn't need one. "I'll have to ask," I say, so he backs the car out and we drive along the main street till we come to a corner store, magazines and candy.

"You must mean the old road," the woman says with only a trace of an accent. "It's been closed for years, what you need is the new one." I buy four vanilla cones because you aren't supposed to ask without buying anything. She gouges down into the cardboard barrel with a metal scoop. Before, the ice cream came rolled in pieces of paper which they would peel off like bark, pressing the short logs of ice cream into the cones with their thumbs. Those must be obsolete.

I go back to the car and tell David the directions. Joe says he likes chocolate better.

Nothing is the same, I don't know the way any more. I slide my tongue around the ice cream, trying to concentrate on it, they put seaweed in it now, but I'm starting to shake, why is the road different, he shouldn't have allowed them to do it, I want to turn around and go back to the city and never find out what happened to him. I'll start crying, that would be horrible, none of them would know what to do and neither would I. I bite down into the cone and I can't feel anything for a minute but the knife-hard pain up the side of my face.

6

Anaesthesia, that's one technique: if it hurts invent a different pain. I'm all right.

David finishes his cone, tossing the carton-flavoured tip out the window, and starts the car. We go through a part that's spread out from the town since I was here, freshly built square bungalows like city ones except for the pink and baby blue trim, and a few oblong shacks further along, tar-paper and bare boards. A clutch of children playing in the wet mud that substitutes for lawns; most of them are dressed in clothes too big for them, which makes them seem stunted.

"They must fuck a lot here," Anna says, "I guess it's the Church." Then she says "Aren't I awful."

David says "The true north strong and free."

Beyond the houses, two older children, darkfaced, hold out tin cans toward the car. Raspberries perhaps.

We come to the gas station where the woman said to turn left and David groans with joy, "Oh god look at that," and they pile out as though it will escape if they aren't quick enough. What they're after is the three stuffed moose on a platform near the pumps: they're dressed in human clothes and wired standing up on their hind legs, a father moose with a trench-coat and a pipe in his mouth, a mother moose in a print dress and flowered hat and a little boy moose in short pants, a striped jersey and a baseball cap, waving an American flag.

Anna and I follow. I go up behind David and say "Don't you need some gas," he shouldn't use the moose without paying, like the washrooms they're here to attract customers.

"Oh look," Anna says, hand going to her mouth, "there's another one on the roof," and there is, a little girl moose in a frilly skirt and a pigtailed blonde wig, holding a red parasol in one hoof. They get her too. The owner of the gas station is standing behind his plateglass show-window in his undershirt, scowling at us through the film of dust.

When we're back in the car I say as though defending myself, "Those weren't here before." Anna's head swivels round, my voice must sound odd.

7

"Before what?" she says.

The new road is paved and straight, two lanes with a line down the middle. Already it's beginning to gather landmarks, a few advertisement signs, a roadside crucifix with a wooden Christ, ribs sticking out, the alien god, mysterious to me as ever. Underneath it are a couple of jam jars with flowers, daisies and red devil's paintbrush and the white ones you can dry, Indian Posies, Everlasting, there must have been a car accident.

At intervals the old road crosses us; it was dirt, full of bumps and potholes, it followed the way the land went, up and down the hills and around the cliffs and boulders. They used to go over it as fast as possible, their father knew every inch of it and could take it (he said) blindfolded, which was what they often seemed to be doing, grinding up past the signs that said PETITE VITESSE and plunging down over the elevator edges and scraping around the rockfaces, GARDEZ LE DROIT, horn hooting; the rest of them clamped onto the inside of the car, getting sicker and sicker despite the Lifesavers their mother would hand out, and finally throwing up groggily by the side of the road, blue asters and pink fireweed, if he could stop in time or out the car window if he couldn't or into paper bags, he anticipated emergencies, if he was in a hurry and didn't want to stop at all.

That won't work, I can't call them "they" as if they were somebody else's family: I have to keep myself from telling that story. Still though, seeing the old road billowing along at a distance through the trees (ruts and traces already blurring with grass and saplings, soon it will be gone) makes me reach into my bag for the Lifesavers I brought. But they aren't needed any more, even though the new road turns from pavement into gravel ("Must've elected the wrong guy last time around," David says jokingly) and the familiar smell of road dust fuming behind and around us mixes with the gas-and-upholstery smell of the car.

"Thought you said this would be bad," David says over his

8

shoulder, "it's not bad at all." We're nearly to the village already, the two roads joining here but widened – rock blasted, trees bulldozed over, roots in the air, needles reddening – past the flat cliff where the election slogans are painted and painted over, some faded and defaced, others fresh yellow and white, VOTEZ GODET, VOTEZ OBRIEN, along with hearts and initials and words and advertisements, THÉ SALADA, BLUE MOON COTTAGES ½ MILE, QUÉBEC LIBRE, FUCK YOU, BUVEZ COCA COLA GLACÉ, JESUS SAVES, mélange of demands and languages, an x-ray of it would be the district's entire history.

But they've cheated, we're here too soon and I feel deprived of something, as though I can't really get here unless I've suffered; as though the first view of the lake, which we can see now, blue and cool as redemption, should be through tears and a haze of vomit.

Chapter Two

We slur down the last hill, gravel pinging off the underside of the car, and suddenly there's a thing that isn't supposed to be here. MOTEL, BAR BIÈRE BEER the sign reads, neon even, someone is trying; but to no avail, there aren't any cars parked outside and the VACANCY notice is up. The building is like any other cheap motel, long grey stucco with aluminum doors; the earth around it is still chunky and raw, not yet overgrown with the road weeds.

"Let's pick up a few," David says, to Joe; he's already swerved the car.

We head towards the door but then I stop, it's the best place to leave them, and say "You go in and have a beer or something, I'll be back in about half an hour."

"Right," David says. He knows what to avoid.

"Want me to come?" Joe offers, but when I say No relief gleams through his beard. The three of them disappear through the screen door of the bar and I walk the rest of the way down the hill.

I like them, I trust them, I can't think of anyone else I like better, but right now I wish they weren't here. Though they're necessary: David's and Anna's car was the only way I could make it, there's no bus and no train and I never hitch. They're doing me a favour, which they disguised by saying it would be fun, they like to travel. But my reason for being here embarrasses them, they don't understand it. They all disowned their parents long ago, the way you are supposed to: Joe never mentions his mother and father, Anna says hers were nothing people and David calls his The Pigs.

There was a covered bridge here once, but it was too far north to be quaint. They tore it down three years before I left, to improve the dam, and replaced it with the concrete bridge which is here now, enormous, monumental, dwarfing the village. It's the dam that controls the lake: sixty years ago they raised the lake level so that whenever they wanted to flush the logs down the narrow outflow river to the mill they would have enough water power. But they don't do much logging here any more. A few men work on railway maintenance, one freight train a day; a couple of families run the stores, the small one where they used to speak English, the other where they wouldn't. The rest process the tourists, businessmen in plaid shirts still creased from the cellophane packages, and wives, if they come, who sit in two's on the screened blackfly-proof porches of the single-room cabins and complain to each other while the men play at fishing.

I pause to lean over the railing on the river side. The flood-gates are open, the froth-coloured and brown rapids topple over the rocks, the sound rushes. The sound is one of the first things I remember, that was what warned them. It was night, I was lying in the bottom of the canoe; they had started out from the village but a heavy fog had risen, so thick they could hardly see the water. They found the shoreline and followed it along; it was dead silent, they could hear what they thought was the howling of wolves, muffled by forest and mist, it meant they had taken the right direction. Then there was the pouring noise of the rapids and they saw where they were, just as the current caught them. They were going backwards, the howling was the village dogs. If the canoe had tipped over we would have been killed, but they were calm, they didn't act like danger; what stayed in my head was only the mist whiteness, the hush of moving water and the rocking motion, total safety.

Anna was right, I had a good childhood; it was in the middle of the war, flecked grey newsreels I never saw, bombs and concentration camps, the leaders roaring at the crowds from inside their uniforms, pain and useless death, flags rippling in time to the anthems. But I didn't know about that till later, when my brother found out and told me. At the time it felt like peace.

Now I'm in the village, walking through it, waiting for the nostalgia to hit, for the cluster of nondescript buildings to be irradiated with inner light like a plug-in crêche, as it has been so often in memory; but nothing happens. It hasn't gotten any bigger, these days the children probably move to the city. The same two-storey frame houses with nasturtiums on the windowsills and squared roof-corners, motley lines of washing trailing from them like the tails of kites; though some of the houses are slicker and have changed colour. The white dollhouse-sized church above on the rock hillside is neglected, peeling paint and a broken window, the old priest must be gone. What I mean is dead.

Down by the shore, a lot of boats are tied up at the government dock but not many cars parked: more boats than cars, a bad season. I try to decide which of the cars is my father's but as I scan them I realize I no longer know what kind of car he would be driving.

I reach the turnoff to Paul's, a rough dirt path rutted by tires, crossing the railroad tracks and continuing through a swamp field, logs laid side by side over the soggy parts. A few black flies catch up with me, it's July, past the breeding time, but as usual there are some left.

The road goes up and I climb it, along the backs of the houses Paul built for his son and his son-in-law and his other son, his clan. Paul's is the original, yellow with maroon trim, squat farmhouse pattern; though this isn't farming country, it's mostly rock and where there's any soil it's thin and sandy.

The closest Paul ever got to farming was to have a cow, killed by the milkbottle. The shed where it and the horses used to live is now a garage.

In the clearing behind the house two 1950s cars are resting, a pink one and a red one, raised on wooden blocks, no wheels; scattered around them are the rusting remains of older cars: like my father, Paul saves everything useful. The house has added a pointed structure like a church spire, made of former car parts welded together; on top of it is a T.V. antenna and on top of that a lightning rod.

Paul is at home, he's in the vegetable garden at the side of the house. He straightens up to watch me, his face leathery and retained as ever, like a closed suitcase; I don't think he knows who I am.

"Bonjour monsieur," I say when I'm at the fence. He takes a step towards me, still guarding, and I say "Don't you remember me," and smile. Again the strangling feeling, paralysis of the throat; but Paul speaks English, he's been outside. "It was very kind of you to write."

"Ah," he says, not recognizing me but deducing who I must be, "Bonjour," and then he smiles too. He clasps his hands in front of him like a priest or a porcelain mandarin; he doesn't say anything else. We stand there on either side of the fence, our faces petrified in well-intentioned curves, mouths wreathed in parentheses, until I say "Has he come back yet?"

At this his chin plummets, his head teeters on his neck. "Ah. No." He gazes sideways, accusingly, down at a potato plant near his left foot. Then his head jerks up again and he says gaily, "Not yet, ay? But maybe soon. Your fadder, he knows the bush."

Madame has appeared in the kitchen doorway and Paul speaks with her in the nasal slanted French I can't interpret because I learned all but a few early words of mine in school. Folk songs and Christmas carols and, from the later grades, memorized passages of Racine and Baudelaire are no help to me here.

"You must come in," he says to me, "and take a tea," and he bends and undoes the hook of the wooden gate. I go forward to the door where Madame is waiting for me, hands outstretched in welcome, smiling and shaking her head mournfully as though through no fault of my own I'm doomed.

Madame makes the tea on a new electric stove, a blue ceramic Madonna with pink child hanging above it; when I glimpsed the stove on my way through the kitchen I felt betrayed, she should have remained loyal to her wood range. We sit on the screened porch overlooking the lake, balancing our teacups and rocking side by side in three rocking chairs; I've been given the store cushion, which has an embroidered view of Niagara Falls. The black and white collie, either the identical one I used to be afraid of or its offshoot, lies on the braided rug by our feet.

Madame, who is the same thickness all the way down, is in a long-skirted dress and black stockings and a print apron with a bib, Paul in high-waisted trousers with braces, flannel shirt-sleeves rolled. I'm annoyed with them for looking so much like carvings, the habitant kind they sell in tourist handicraft shops; but of course it's the other way around, it's the carvings that look like them. I wonder what they think I look like, they may find my jeans and sweatshirt and fringed over-the-shoulder bag strange, perhaps immoral, though such things may be more common in the village since the tourists and the T.V.; besides, I can be forgiven because my family was, by reputation, peculiar as well as *anglais*.

I lift my cup, they are watching me anxiously: it's imperative that I mention the tea. "Très bon," I manage to get out in the direction of Madame. "Délicieux." Doubt seizes me, *thé* may be feminine.

What I'm remembering are the visits our mother was obliged to pay Madame while our father was visiting Paul. My father and Paul would be outside, talking about boats or motors or forest fires or one of their expeditions, and my mother and Madame would be inside in the rocking chairs (my mother with the Niagara Falls cushion), trying with great goodwill to make conversation. Neither knew more than five words of the other's language and after the opening Bonjours both would unconsciously raise their voices as though talking to a deaf person.

"Il fait beau," my mother would shout, no matter what the weather was like, and Madame would grin with strain and say "Pardon? Ah, il fait *beau*, oui, il fait beau, ban oui." When she had ground to a stop both would think desperately, chairs rocking.

" 'Ow are *you*?" Madame would scream, and my mother, after deciphering this, would say "*Fine*, I am fine." Then she would repeat the question: "How are *you*, Madame?" But Madame would not have the answer and both, still smiling, would glance furtively out through the screen to see if the men were yet coming to rescue them.

Meanwhile my father would be giving Paul the cabbages or the string beans he had brought from his garden and Paul would be replying with tomatoes or lettuces from his. Since their gardens had the same things in them this exchange of vegetables was purely ritual: after it had taken place we would know the visit would be officially over.

Madame is stirring her tea now and sighing. She says something to Paul and Paul says, "Your mother, she was a good woman, Madame says it is very sad; so young too."

"Yes," I say. Mother and Madame were about the same age and no-one would call Madame young; but then my mother never got fat like Madame.

I went to see her in the hospital, where she allowed herself to be taken only when she could no longer walk; one of the doctors told me that. She must have concealed the pain for weeks, tricked my father into believing it was only one of her usual headaches, that would be her kind of lie. She hated hospitals and doctors; she must have been afraid they would experiment on her, keep her alive as long as they could with tubes and needles even though it was what they call terminal,

15

in the head it always is; and in fact that's what they did.

They had her on morphine, she said there were webs floating in the air in front of her. She was very thin, much older
than I'd ever thought possible, skin tight over her curved beak
nose, hands on the sheet curled like bird claws clinging to a
perch. She peered at me with bright blank eyes. She may not
have known who I was: she didn't ask me why I left or where
I'd been, though she might not have asked anyway, feeling as
she always had that personal questions were rude.

"I'm not going to your funeral," I said. I had to lean close
to her, the hearing in one of her ears was gone. I wanted her
to understand in advance, and approve.

"I never enjoyed them," she said to me, one word at a time.
"You have to wear a hat. I don't like liquor." She must have
been talking about Church or cocktail parties. She lifted her
hand, slowly as if through water, and felt the top of her head;
there was a tuft of white hair standing straight up. "I didn't
get the bulbs in. Is there snow outside?"

On the bedside table with the flowers, chrysanthemums, I
saw her diary; she kept one every year. All she put in it was a
record of the weather and the work done on that day: no re-
flections, no emotions. She would refer to it when she wanted
to compare the years, decide whether the spring had been late
or early, whether it had been a wet summer. It made me angry
to see it in that windowless room where it was no use; I waited
till her eyes were closed and slipped it into my shoulder bag.
When I got outside I leafed through it, I thought there might
be something about me, but except for the dates the pages
were blank, she had given up months ago.

"Do what you think best," she said from behind her closed
eyes. "Is there snow?"

We rock some more. I want to ask Paul about my father
but he ought to begin, he must have news to tell me. Maybe
he's avoiding it; or maybe he's being tactful, waiting until
I'm ready. Finally I say "What happened to him?"

Paul shrugs. "He is just gone," he says. "I go there one day to see him, the door is open, the boats is there, I think maybe he is off somewheres near, and I wait awhile. Next day I go back, everything the same, I begin to worry, where he is, I don't know. So I write to you, he has leaved your *caisse postale* and the keys, I lock up the place. His car she is here, with me." He gestures towards the back, the garage. My father trusted Paul, he said Paul could build anything and fix anything. They were once caught in a three-week rainstorm, my father said if you could spend three weeks in a wet tent with a man without killing him or having him kill you then he was a good man. Paul justified for him his own ideal of the simple life; but for Paul the anachronism was imposed, he'd never chosen it.

"Did you look on the island?" I say. "If the boats are there he can't have gone off the island."

"I look, sure," Paul says, "I tell the police from down-the-road, they look around, nobody find nothing. Your husband here too?" he asks irrelevantly.

"Yes, he's here," I say, skipping over the lie even in my own mind. What he means is that a man should be handling this; Joe will do as a stand-in. My status is a problem, they obviously think I'm married. But I'm safe, I'm wearing my ring, I never threw it out, it's useful for landladies. I sent my parents a postcard after the wedding, they must have mentioned it to Paul; that, but not the divorce. It isn't part of the vocabulary here, there's no reason to upset them.

I'm waiting for Madame to ask about the baby, I'm prepared, alerted, I'll tell her I left him in the city; that would be perfectly true, only it was a different city, he's better off with my husband, former husband.

But Madame doesn't mention it, she lifts another cube of sugar from the tray by her side and he intrudes, across from me, a coffee shop, not city but roadside, on the way to or from somewhere, some goal or encounter. He peels the advertisement paper from the sugar and lets one square fall into the cup, I'm talking and his mouth turns indulgent, it must have been before the child. He smiles and I smile too, thinking of the slice of cucumber pickle that was stuck to the top of his club sandwich. A round historical plaque, on a supermarket wall or in a parking lot, marking the site where a building once stood in which an event of little importance once took place, ridiculous. He puts his hand on mine, he tries that a lot but he's easy to get rid of, easier and easier. I don't have time for him, I switch problems.

I sip at my tea and rock, by my feet the dog stirs, the lake below flutters in the wind which is beginning. My father has simply disappeared then, vanished into nothing. When I got Paul's letter – "Your father is gone, nobody cant find him" – it seemed incredible, but it appears to be true.

There used to be a barometer on the porch wall, a wooden house with two doors and a man and a woman who lived inside. When it was going to be fair the woman in her long skirt and apron would emerge from her door, when it was going to rain she would go in and the man would come out, carrying an axe. When it was first explained to me I thought they controlled the weather instead of merely responding to it. My eyes seek the house now, I need a prediction, but it's not there.

"I think I'll go down the lake," I say.

Paul raises his hands, palms outward. "We look two, three times already."

But they must have missed something, I feel it will be different if I look myself. Probably when we get there my father will have returned from wherever he has been, he will be sitting in the cabin waiting for us.

Chapter Three

On my way back to the motel I detour to the store, the one where they're supposed to speak English: we will need some food. I go up the wooden steps, past a drowsing mop-furred mongrel roped to the porch with a length of clothesline. The screen door has a BLACK CAT CIGARETTES handle; I open it and step into the store smell, the elusive sweetish odour given off by the packaged cookies and the soft drink cooler. For a brief time the post office was here, a DEFENSE DE CRACHER SUR LE PLANCHER sign stamped with a government coat of arms.

Behind the counter there's a woman about my age, but with brassiere-shaped breasts and a light auburn moustache; her hair is in rollers covered by a pink net and she has on slacks and a sleeveless jersey top. The old priest is definitely gone, he disapproved of slacks, the women had to wear long concealing skirts and dark stockings and keep their arms covered in church. Shorts were against the law, and many of them lived all their lives beside the lake without learning to swim because they were ashamed to put on bathing suits.

The woman looks at me, inquisitive but not smiling, and the two men still in Elvis Presley haircuts, duck's ass at the back and greased pompadours curving out over their foreheads, stop talking and look at me too; they keep their elbows on the counter. I hesitate: maybe the tradition has changed, maybe they no longer speak English.

"Avez-vous du viande hâché?" I ask her, blushing because of my accent.

She grins then and the two men grin also, not at me but at each other. I see I've made a mistake, I should have pretended to be an American.

"Amburger, oh yes we have lots. *H*ow much?" she asks, adding the final H carelessly to show she can if she feels like it. This is border country.

"A pound, no two pounds," I say, blushing even more because I've been so easily discovered, they're making fun of me and I have no way of letting them know I share the joke. Also I agree with them, if you live in a place you should speak the language. But this isn't where I lived.

She hacks with a cleaver at a cube of frozen meat, weighs it. "Doo leevers," she says, mimicking my school accent. The two men snigger. I solace myself by replaying the man from the government, he was at a gallery opening, a handicraft exhibit, string wall hangings, woven place mats, stoneware breakfast sets; Joe wanted to go so he could resent not being in it. The man seemed to be a cultural attaché of some sort, an ambassador; I asked him if he knew this part of the country, my part, and he shook his head and said "Des barbares, they are not civilized." At the time that annoyed me.

I pick up some fly dope in a spray can for the others, also some eggs and bacon, bread and butter, miscellaneous tins. Everything is more expensive here than in the city; no one keeps hens or cows or pigs any more, it's all imported from more fertile districts. The bread is in wax paper wrappers, tranché.

I would like to back out the door, I don't want them staring at me from behind; but I force myself to walk slowly, frontwards.

There used to be only one store. It was in the front part of a house, run by an old woman who was also called Madame:

none of the women had names then. Madame sold khaki-coloured penny candies which we were forbidden to eat, but her main source of power was that she had only one hand. Her other arm ended in a soft pink snout like an elephant's trunk and she broke the parcel string by wrapping it around her stump and pulling. This arm devoid of a hand was for me a great mystery, almost as puzzling as Jesus. I wanted to know how the hand had come off (perhaps she had taken it off herself) and where it was now, and especially whether my own hand could ever come off like that; but I never asked, I must have been afraid of the answers. Going down the steps, I try to remember what the rest of her was like, her face, but I can see only the potent candies, inaccessible in their glass reliquary, and the arm, miraculous in an unspecified way like the toes of saints or the cut-off pieces of early martyrs, the eyes on the plate, the severed breasts, the heart with letters on it shining like a light bulb through the trim hole painted in the chest, art history.

I find the others in the small chilly room labelled BAR; they're the only customers. They have six beer bottles and four glasses on their orange formica-topped table. A mottled boy with a haircut like the ones of the men in the store, only blonde, is sitting with them.

David waves at me as I come in: he's happy about something. "Have a beer," he says. "This is Claude, his father owns this joint."

Claude shambles off morosely to get me a beer. Underneath the bar itself is a crudely carved wooden fish with red and blue dots on it, intended possibly for a speckled trout; on its leaping back it supports the fake marble surface. Above the bar is a T.V., turned off or broken, and the regulation picture, scrolled gilt frame, blown-up photograph of a stream with trees and rapids and a man fishing. It's an imitation of other places, more southern ones, which are themselves imitations, the original someone's distorted memory of a nineteenth century English gentleman's shooting lodge, the kind with trophy heads and furniture made from deer antlers, Queen Victoria had a set like that. But if this is what succeeds why shouldn't they do it?

"Claude told us business is bad this year," David says, "on accounta word is around the lake's fished out. They're going to other lakes, Claude's dad flies them in his seaplane, neat eh? But he says some of the men went out in the spring with a dragnet and there's all kinds of them down there, real big ones, they're just gettin' too smart." David is slipping into his yokel dialect; he does it for fun, it's a parody of himself, the way he says he talked back in the fifties when he wanted to be a minister and was selling Bibles door-to-door to put himself through theological seminary: "Hey lady, wanna buy a dirty book?" Now though it seems to be unconscious, maybe he's doing it for Claude, to make it clear he too is a man of the people. Or maybe it's an experiment in Communications, that's what he teaches, at night, the same place Joe works; it's an Adult Education programme. David calls it Adult Vegetation; he got the job because he was once a radio announcer.

"Any news?" Joe asks, in a neutral mumble that signals he'd prefer it if I kept from showing any reaction, no matter what has happened.

"No," I say, "Nothing different." Voice level, calm. Perhaps that was what he liked about me, there must have been something, though I can't reconstruct our first meeting, now I can: it was in a store, I was buying some new brushes and a spray tin of fixative. He said Do you live around here and we went to the corner for a coffee, except I had a 7-up instead. What impressed him that time, he even mentioned it later, cool he called it, was the way I took off my clothes and put them on again later very smoothly as if I were feeling no emotion. But I really wasn't.

Claude comes back with the beer and I say "Thank you" and glance up at him and his face dissolves and re-forms, he was about eight the last time I was here; he used to peddle worms in rusted tin cans to the fishermen down by the government dock. He's uneasy now, he can tell I recognize him.

"I'd like to go down the lake for a couple of days," I say, to David because it's his car. "I'd like to look around, if that's okay."

"Great," says David, "I'm gonna get me one of them smart fish." He brought along a borrowed fishing rod, though I warned him he might not have a chance to use it: if my father had turned up after all we would have gone away without letting him find out we were here. If he's safe I don't want to see him. There's no point, they never forgave me, they didn't understand the divorce; I don't think they even understood the marriage, which wasn't surprising since I didn't understand it myself. What upset them was the way I did it, so suddenly, and then running off and leaving my husband and child, my attractive full-colour magazine illustrations, suitable for framing. Leaving my child, that was the unpardonable sin; it was no use trying to explain to them why it wasn't really mine. But I admit I was stupid, stupidity is the same as evil if you judge by the results, and I didn't have any excuses, I was never good at them. My brother was, he used to make them up in advance of the transgressions; that's the logical way.

"Oh god," Anna says, "David thinks he's a great white hunter." She's teasing him, she does that a lot; but he doesn't hear, he's getting up, Claude is hustling him off to make him out a licence, it seems Claude is in charge of the licences. When David comes back I want to ask how much he paid, but he's too pleased, I don't want to spoil it. Claude is pleased also.

We find out from Claude we can hire Evans, who owns the Blue Moon Cabins, to run us down the lake. Paul would take us for nothing, he offered, but I wouldn't feel right about it; also I'm sure he would misinterpret Joe's amorphous beard and David's moustache and Three Musketeers hair. They're just a style now, like crew cuts, but Paul might feel they are dangerous, they mean riots.

David eases the car down the turnoff, two ruts and a rock hump in the centre that scrapes the car's belly. We brake in front of the cabin marked OFFICE; Evans is there, a bulky laconic American in checked shirt and peaked cap and a thick knitted jacket with an eagle on the back. He knows where my father's place is, all the older guides know every house on the lake. He moves his cigarette butt to the corner of his mouth and says he'll take us there, ten miles, for five dollars; for another five he'll pick us up two days from now, in the morning. That will give us the rest of the day to drive back to the city. He's heard of the disappearance, of course, but he doesn't mention it.

"A groovy old guy, eh?" David says when we're outside. He's enjoying himself, he thinks this is reality: a marginal economy and grizzled elderly men, it's straight out of Depression photo essays. He spent four years in New York and became political, he was studying something; it was during the sixties, I'm not sure when. My friends' pasts are vague to me and to each other also, any one of us could have amnesia for years and the others wouldn't notice.

When David has backed the car down to the Blue Moon dock we unload our stuff, the packsacks of clothes, the camera equipment, the samsonite case with my career in it, the half dozen Red Caps they got at the motel and the paper bag of food. We scramble into the boat, a battered wood-hulled launch; Evans starts the motor and we churn out slowly. Summer cottages beginning to sprout here, they spread like measles, it must be the paved road.

David sits in front beside Evans. "Gettin' many fish?" he asks, folksy, chummy, crafty. "Here and there, here and there," Evans says, giving no free handouts; then he switches the motor into high gear and I can't hear any more.

I wait until we're into the middle of the lake. At the right moment I look over my shoulder as I always did and there is the village, suddenly distanced and clear, the houses receding and grouping, the white church startling against the dark of the trees. The feeling I expected before but failed to have comes now, homesickness, for a place where I never lived, I'm far enough away; then the village shrinks, optical illusion, and we're around a point of land, it's behind us.

The three of us are together on the back seat, Anna beside me. "This is good," she says to me, voice shrilling over the engine roar, "it's good for us to get away from the city"; but when I turn to answer there are tears on her cheek and I wonder why, she's always so cheerful. Then I realize they aren't tears, it's started to drizzle. The raincoats are in our packsacks; I didn't notice it had clouded over. We won't be very wet though, with this boat it will only take half an hour; before, with the heavier boats and primitive motors, it took two to three hours depending on the wind. In the city people would say to my mother, "Aren't you afraid? What if something happened?" They were thinking of the time it would take to get to a doctor.

I'm cold, I huddle my shoulders up; drops ping onto my skin. The shoreline unrolls and folds together again as we go past; forty miles from here there's another village, in between there's nothing but a tangled maze, low hills curving out of the water, bays branching in, peninsulas which turn into islands, islands, necks of land leading to other lakes. On a map or in an aerial photograph the water pattern radiates like a spider, but in a boat you can see only a small part of it, the part you're in.

The lake is tricky, the weather shifts, the wind swells up quickly; people drown every year, boats loaded topheavy or drunken fishermen running at high speed into deadheads, old pieces of tree waterlogged and partly decayed, floating under the surface, there are a lot of them left over from the logging and the time they raised the lake level. Because of the convolutions it's easy to lose the way if you haven't memorized the landmarks and I watch for them now, dome-shaped hill, point with dead pine, stubble of cut trunks poking up from a shallows, I don't trust Evans.

But he's taken the right turns so far, we're coming into my territory, two short bends and through a passage between granite shores and out into a wider bay. The peninsula is where I left it, pushing out from the island shore with the house not even showing through the trees, though I know where it is; camouflage was one of my father's policies.

Evans arches the boat around the point and slows for the dock. The dock slants, the ice takes something away from it every winter and the water warps and rots it; it's been repaired so much all the materials are different, but it's the same dock my brother fell off the time he drowned.

He used to be kept in a chicken-wire enclosure my father built for him, large cage or small playground, with trees, a swing, rocks, a sandpile. The fence was too high for him to climb over but there was a gate and one day he learned how to open it. My mother was alone in the house; she glanced out the window, checking, and he was no longer in the cage. It was a still day, no wind noise, and she heard something down by the water. She ran to the dock, he wasn't there, she went out to the end of it and looked down. My brother was under the water, face upturned, eyes open and unconscious, sinking gently; air was coming out of his mouth.

It was before I was born but I can remember it as clearly as if I saw it, and perhaps I did see it: I believe that an unborn baby has its eyes open and can look out through the walls of the mother's stomach, like a frog in a jar.

Chapter Four

We unload our baggage while Evans idles the motor. When David has paid him he gives us an uninterested nod and backs the boat out, then turns it and swings around the point, the sound dwindling to a whine and fading as land and distance move between us. The lake jiggles against the shore, the waves subside, nothing remains but a faint iridescent film of gasoline, purple and pink and green. The space is quiet, the wind has gone down and the lake is flat, silver-white, it's the first time all day (and for a long time, for years) we have been out of the reach of motors. My ears and body tingle, aftermath of the vibration, like feet taken out of roller-skates.

The others are standing aimlessly; they seem to be waiting for me to tell them what comes next. "We'll take the things up," I say. I warn them about the dock: it's slippery with the drizzle, which is lighter now, almost a mist; also some of the boards may be soft and treacherous.

What I want to do is shout "Hello!" or "We're here!" but I don't, I don't want to hear the absence.

I hoist a packsack and walk along the dock and onto the land and towards the cabin, following the path and climbing the steps set into the hillside, lengths of split cedar held in place by a stake pounded at each end. The house is built on a sand hill, part of a ridge left by the retreating glaciers; only a few inches of soil and a thin coating of trees hold it down.

On the lake side the sand is exposed, raw, it's been crumbling away: the stones and charcoal from the fireplace they used when they first lived here in tents have long since vanished, and the edge trees fall gradually, several I remember upright are leaning now. Red pines, bark scaling, needles bunched on the top branches. A kingfisher is perched on one of them, making its staccato alarm-clock cry; they nest in the cliff, burrowing into the sand, it speeds up the erosion.

In front of the house the chicken-wire fence is still here, though one end is almost over the brink. They never dismantled it; even the dwarf swing is there, ropes frayed, sagging and blotched with weather. It wasn't like them to keep something when it was no longer needed; perhaps they expected grandchildren, visiting here. He would have wanted a dynasty, like Paul's, houses and descendants proliferating around him. The fence is a reproach, it points to my failure.

But I couldn't have brought the child here, I never identified it as mine; I didn't name it before it was born even, the way you're supposed to. It was my husband's, he imposed it on me, all the time it was growing in me I felt like an incubator. He measured everything he would let me eat, he was feeding it on me, he wanted a replica of himself; after it was born I was no more use. I couldn't prove it though, he was clever: he kept saying he loved me.

The house is smaller, because (I realize) the trees around it have grown. It's turned greyer in nine years too, like hair. The cedar logs are upright instead of horizontal, upright logs are shorter and easier for one man to handle. Cedar isn't the best wood, it decays quickly. Once my father said "I didn't build it to last forever" and I thought then, Why not? Why didn't you?

I hope the door will be open but it's padlocked, as Paul said he left it. I dig the keys he gave me out of my bag and approach warily: whatever I find inside will be a clue. What if he returned after Paul locked it and couldn't get in? But there are other ways of getting in, he could have broken a window.

Joe and David are here now with the other packsacks

and the beer. Anna is behind them with my case and the paper bag; she's singing again, Mockingbird Hill.

I open the wooden door and the screen door inside it and scan the room cautiously, then step inside. Table covered with blue oilcloth, bench, another bench which is a wooden box built against the wall, sofa with metal frame and thin mattress, it folds out into a bed. That was where our mother used to be: all day she would lie unmoving, covered with a brown plaid blanket, her face bloodless and shrunken. We would talk in whispers, she looked so different and she didn't hear if we spoke to her; but the next day she would be the same as she had always been. We came to have faith in her ability to recover, from anything; we ceased to take her illnesses seriously, they were only natural phases, like cocoons. When she died I was disappointed in her.

Nothing is out of place. Water drops fall on the roof, down from the trees.

They follow me inside. "Is this where you lived?" Joe asks. It's unusual for him to ask me anything about myself: I can't tell whether he's pleased or discouraged. He goes over to the snowshoes on the wall and lifts one down, taking refuge in his hands.

Anna puts the groceries on the counter and wraps her arms around herself. "It must have been weird," she says. "Cut off from everything like that."

"No," I say. To me it felt normal.

"Depends what you're used to," David says. "I think it's neat." But he's not certain.

There are two other rooms and I open the doors quickly. A bed in each, shelves, clothes hanging on nails: jackets, raincoats, they were always left here. A grey hat, he had several of those. In the right-hand room is a map of the district, tacked to the wall. In the other are some pictures, watercolours, I recall now having painted them when I was twelve or thirteen; the fact that I'd forgotten about them is the only thing that makes me uneasy.

I go back to the livingroom. David has dropped his packsack on the floor and unfolded himself along the sofa. "Christ, am I wiped," he says. "Somebody break me out a beer." Anna brings him one and he pats her on the rear and says "That's what I like, service." She takes out cans for herself and us and we sit on the benches and drink it. Now that we're no longer moving the cabin is chilly.

The right smell, cedar and wood stove and tar from the oakum stuffed between the logs to keep out the mice. I look up at the ceiling, the shelves: there's a stack of papers beside the lamp, perhaps he was working on them just before whatever it was happened, before he left. There might be something for me, a note, a message, a will. I kept expecting that after my mother died, word of some kind, not money but an object, a token. For a while I went twice a day to the post office box which was the only one of my addresses I'd given them; but nothing arrived, maybe she didn't have time.

No dirty dishes, no clothing strewn around, no evidence. It doesn't feel like a house that's been lived in all winter.

"What time is it?" I ask David. He holds up his watch: it's almost five. It will be up to me to organize dinner, since in a way this is my place, they are my guests.

There's kindling in the box behind the stove and a few pieces of white birch; the disease hasn't yet hit this part of the country. I find the matches and kneel in front of the stove, I've almost forgotten how to do this but after three or four matches I get it lit.

I take the round enamelled bowl down from its hook and the big knife. They watch me: none of them asks me where I'm going, though Joe seems worried. Perhaps he's been expecting me to have hysterics and he's anxious because I'm not having any. "I'm going to the garden," I say to reassure them. They know where that is, they could see it from the lake coming in.

Grass is growing up in the path and in front of the gate; the weeds are a month tall. Ordinarily I would spend a few hours pulling them out, but it isn't worth it, we'll be here only two days.

Frogs hop everywhere out of my way, they like it here; it's close to the lake, damp, my canvas shoes are soaked through. I pick some of the leaf lettuce that hasn't flowered and turned bitter, then I pull up an onion, sliding the loose brown outer skin off from the bulb, white and eye-like.

The garden's been rearranged: before there were scarlet runners up one side of the fence. The blossoms were redder than anything else in the garden, the hummingbirds went into them, hovering, their wings a blur. The beans that were left too long would yellow after the first frost and split open. Inside were pebbles, purple-black and frightening. I knew that if I could get some of them and keep them for myself I would be all-powerful; but later when I was tall enough and could finally reach to pick them it didn't work. Just as well, I think, as I had no idea what I would do with the power once I got it; if I'd turned out like the others with power I would have been evil.

I go to the carrot row and pull up a carrot but they haven't been thinned properly, it's forked and stubby. I cut off the onion leaves and the carrot top and throw them on the compost heap, then put the things in the bowl and start back towards the gate, adding up the time, growing time, in my head. In the middle of June he was here surely, it can't be longer than that.

Anna is outside the fence, she's come to look for me. "Where's the can?" she says. "I'm about to burst."

I take her to the beginning of the trail and point her along it.

"Are you okay?" she says.

"Sure," I say; the question surprises me.

"I'm sorry he wasn't here," she says mournfully, gazing at me out of her round green eyes as though it's her grief, her catastrophe.

"It's all right," I tell her, comforting her, "just keep going along the path and you'll find it, though it's quite a distance," I laugh, "don't get lost."

I carry the bowl down to the dock and wash the vegetables

31

in the lake. Below me in the water there's a leech, the good kind with red dots on the back, undulating along like a streamer held at one end and shaken. The bad kind is mottled grey and yellow. It was my brother who made up these moral distinctions, at some point he became obsessed with them, he must have picked them up from the war. There had to be a good kind and a bad kind of everything.

I cook the hamburgers and we eat and I wash the dishes in the chipped dishpan, Anna drying; then it's almost dark. I lift the bedding out from the wall bench and make up our bed, Anna can do theirs. He must have been sleeping in the main room, on the sofa.

They aren't used to going to bed as soon as it's dark though, and neither am I any more. I'm afraid they'll be bored because there's no T.V. or anything, I search for entertainments. A box of dominoes, a deck of cards, those were under the folded blankets. There are a lot of paperbacks on the shelves in the bedrooms, detective novels mostly, recreational reading. Beside them are the technical books on trees and the other reference books, *Edible Plants and Shoots*, *Tying the Dry Fly*, *The Common Mushrooms*, *Log Cabin Construction*, *A Field Guide to the Birds*, *Exploring Your Camera*, he believed that with the proper guide books you could do everything yourself; and his cache of serious books: the King James Bible which he said he enjoyed for its literary qualities, a complete Robert Burns, Boswell's *Life*, Thompson's *Seasons*, selections from Goldsmith and Cowper. He admired what he called the eighteenth century rationalists: he thought of them as men who had avoided the corruptions of the Industrial Revolution and learned the secret of the golden mean, the balanced life, he was sure they all practised organic farming. It astounded me to discover much later, in fact my husband told me, that Burns was an alcoholic, Cowper a madman, Doctor Johnson a manic-depressive and Goldsmith a pauper. There was something wrong with Thompson also; "escapist" was the term he used. After that I liked them better, they weren't paragons any more.

"I'll light the lamp," I say, "and we can read."

But David says "Naaa, why read when you can do that in the city?" He's twiddling the dial on his transistor radio; he can't pick up anything but static and a wail that might be music, wavering in and out, and a tiny insect voice whispering in French. "Shit," he says, "I wish I could get the scores." He means baseball, he's a fan.

"We could play bridge," I say, but no one wants to.

After a while David says "Well children, time to break out the grass." He opens his packsack and gropes around inside, and Anna says "What a dumb place to put them, it's the first place they'd look."

"Up your ass," David says, smiling at her, "that's where they'd look first, they grab a good thing when they see one. Don't worry, baby, I know what I'm doing."

"Sometimes I wonder," Anna says.

We go outside and down to the dock and sit on the damp wood, watching the sunset, smoking a little. The clouds to the west are yellow and grey, fading, and in the clear sky southeast of us the moon is rising.

"This is great," David says, "it's better than in the city. If we could only kick out the fascist pig Yanks and the capitalists this would be a neat country. But then, who would be left?"

"Oh Christ," Anna says, "don't get going on that."

"How?" I say. "How would you kick them out?"

"Organize the beavers," David says, "chew them to pieces, it's the only way. This Yank stockbroker is going along Bay Street and the beavers ambush him, drop on him from a telephone pole, chomp chomp and it's all over. You heard about the latest national flag? Nine beavers pissing on a frog."

It's old and shoddy but I laugh anyway. A little beer, a little pot, some jokes, a little political chitchat, the golden mean; we're the new bourgeoisie, this might as well be a Rec Room. Still I'm glad they're with me, I wouldn't want to be here alone; at any moment the loss, vacancy, will overtake me, they ward it off.

"Do you realize," David says, "that this country is founded

on the bodies of dead animals? Dead fish, dead seals, and historically dead beavers, the beaver is to this country what the black man is to the United States. Not only that, in New York it's now a dirty word, beaver. I think that's very significant." He sits up and glares at me through the semi-darkness.

"We aren't your students," Anna says, "lie down." His head rests in her lap, she's stroking his forehead, I can see her hand moving back and forth. They've been married nine years, Anna told me, they must have got married about the same time I did; but she's older than I am. They must have some special method, formula, some knowledge I missed out on; or maybe he was the wrong person. I thought it would happen without my doing anything about it, I'd turn into part of a couple, two people linked together and balancing each other, like the wooden man and woman in the barometer house at Paul's. It was good at first but he changed after I married him, he married me, we committed that paper act. I still don't see why signing a name should make any difference but he began to expect things, he wanted to be pleased. We should have kept sleeping together and left it at that.

Joe puts his arm around me, I take hold of his fingers. What I'm seeing is the black and white tugboat that used to be on the lake, or was it flat like a barge, it towed the log booms slowly down towards the dam, I waved at it whenever we went past in our boat and the men would wave back. It had a little house on it for them to live in, with windows and a stovepipe coming out through the roof. I felt that would be the best way to live, in a floating house carrying everything you needed with you and some other people you liked; when you wanted to move somewhere else it would be easy.

Joe is swaying back and forth, rocking, which may mean he's happy. The wind starts again, brushing over us, the air warm-cool and fluid, the trees behind us moving their leaves, the sound ripples; the water gives off icy light, zinc moon breaking on small waves. Loon voice, each hair on my body lifting with the shiver; the echoes deflect from all sides, surrounding us, here everything echoes.

Chapter Five

Birdsong wakes me. It's pre-dawn, earlier than the traffic starts in the city, but I've learned to sleep through that. I used to know the species; I listen, my ears are rusty, there's nothing but a jumble of sound. They sing for the same reason trucks honk, to proclaim their territories: a rudimentary language. Linguistics, I should have studied that instead of art.

Joe is half-awake too and groaning to himself, the sheet pulled around his head like a cowl. He's torn the blankets up from the bottom of the bed and his lean feet stick out, toes with the deprived look of potatoes sprouted in the bag. I wonder if he'll remember he woke me when it was still dark, sitting up and saying "Where is this?" Every time we're in a new place he does that. "It's all right," I said, "I'm here," and though he said "Who? Who?", repeating it like an owl, he allowed me to ease him back down into bed. I'm afraid to touch him at these times, he might mistake me for one of the enemies in his nightmare; but he's beginning to trust my voice.

I examine the part of his face that shows, an eyelid and the side of his nose, the skin pallid as though he's been living in a cellar, which we have been; his beard is dark brown, almost black, it continues around his neck and merges under the sheet with the hair on his back. His back is hairier than most men's, a warm texture, it's like teddy-bear fur, though when

35

I told him that he seemed to take it as an insult to his dignity.

I'm trying to decide whether or not I love him. It shouldn't matter, but there's always a moment when curiosity becomes more important to them than peace and they need to ask; though he hasn't yet. It's best to have the answer worked out in advance: whether you evade or do it the hard way and tell the truth, at least you aren't caught off guard. I sum him up, dividing him into categories: he's good in bed, better than the one before; he's moody but he's not much bother, we split the rent and he doesn't talk much, that's an advantage. When he suggested we should live together I didn't hesitate. It wasn't even a real decision, it was more like buying a goldfish or a potted cactus plant, not because you want one in advance but because you happen to be in the store and you see them lined up on the counter. I'm fond of him, I'd rather have him around than not; though it would be nice if he meant something more to me. The fact that he doesn't makes me sad: no one has since my husband. A divorce is like an amputation, you survive but there's less of you.

I lie for a while with my eyes open. This used to be my room; Anna and David are in the one with the map, this one has the pictures. Ladies in exotic costumes, sausage rolls of hair across their foreheads, with puffed red mouths and eyelashes like toothbrush bristles: when I was ten I believed in glamour, it was a kind of religion and these were my icons. Their arms and legs are constrained in fashion-model poses, one gloved hand on the hip, one foot stuck out in front. They're wearing shoes with Petunia Pig toes and perpendicular heels, and their dresses have cantaloupe strapless tops like Rita Hayworth's and ballerina skirts with blotches meant for spangles. I didn't draw very well then, there's something wrong with the proportions, the necks are too short and the shoulders are enormous. I must have been imitating the paper dolls they had in the city, cardboard movie stars, Jane Powell, Esther Williams, with two-piece bathing suits printed on their bodies and cutout wardrobes of formal gowns and lacy negligées. Little girls in grey jumpers and white blouses, braids clipped to their heads with pink plastic barrettes, owned and directed them; they would bring them to school and parade them at recess, propping them up against the worn brick wall, feet in the snow, paper dresses no protection against the icy wind, inventing for them dances and parties, celebrations, interminable changing of costumes, a slavery of pleasure.

Below the pictures at the foot of the bed there's a grey leather jacket hanging on a nail. It's dirty and the leather is cracked and peeling. I see it for a while before I recognize it: it belonged to my mother a long time ago, she kept sunflower seeds in the pockets. I thought she'd thrown it out; it shouldn't still be here, he should have got rid of it after the funeral. Dead people's clothes ought to be buried with them.

I turn over and shove Joe further against the wall so I can curl up.

I surface again later; Joe is wide awake now, he's come out from under the sheet. "You talked in your sleep again," I tell him. Sometimes I think he says more when he's asleep than he does when he's awake.

He gives a noncommittal growl. "I'm hungry." Then, after a pause, "What did I say?"

"The usual. You wanted to know where you were and who I was." I'd like to hear about the dream itself; I used to have dreams but I don't any longer.

"That's pretty boring," he says. "Was that all?"

I throw back the covers and lower my feet to the floor, a minor ordeal: even in midsummer here the nights are cold. I get dressed as fast as possible and go out to start the fire. Anna is there, still in her sleeveless nylon nightgown and bare feet, standing in front of the wavery yellowish mirror. There's a zippered case on the counter in front of her, she's putting on makeup. I realize I've never seen her without it before; shorn of the pink cheeks and heightened eyes her face is curiously battered, a worn doll's, her artificial face is the natural one. The backs of her arms have goose pimples.

"You don't need that here," I say, "there's no one to look at you." My mother's phrase, used to me once when I was fourteen; she was watching, dismayed, as I covered my mouth with Tango Tangerine. I told her I was just practising.

Anna says in a low voice, "He doesn't like to see me without it," and then, contradicting herself, "He doesn't know I wear it." I glimpse the subterfuge this must involve, or is it devotion: does she have to sneak out of the bed before he's awake every morning and into it at night with the lights out? Maybe David is telling generous lies; but she blends and mutes herself so well he may not notice.

While the stove is heating I go outside, first up to the outhouse and down again to the lake to dip my hands and face, then to the refrigerator, a metal garbage can sunk in the ground with a tight-fitting raccoon-proof lid and over that a heavy wooden cover. When the game wardens arrived in their police launch, as they did once a year, they could never believe we didn't have an icebox, they used to search everywhere for hidden, illegal fish.

I reach down for the eggs; the bacon is in a screened box under the cabin, ventilated but protected from flies and mice. In a settler's house these would have been rootcellar and smoke-house; my father is an improvisor on standard themes.

I carry the food inside and start the breakfast. Joe and David are up, Joe sitting on the wall bench, face still fuzzy with sleep, David examining his chin in the mirror.

"I can make you hot water if you want to shave," I suggest, but his reflection grins and he shakes his head.

"Naaa," he says, "I'm gonna grow me a little old beard."

"Don't you dare," Anna says. "I don't like him kissing me when he has a beard, it reminds me of a cunt." Her hand goes over her mouth as though she is shocked. "Isn't that awful?"

"Filthy talk, woman," David says, "she's uncultured and vulgar."

"Oh I know. I've always been like that."

It's a quick skit, Joe and I are the audience, but Joe is still off in the place inside himself where he spends most of his time and I'm at the stove turning the bacon, I can't watch them so they stop.

I crouch down in front of the stove and open the firebox door to make the toast over the coals. There are no dirty words any more, they've been neutered, now they're only parts of speech; but I recall the feeling, puzzled, baffled, when I found out some words were dirty and the rest were clean. The bad ones in French are the religious ones, the worst ones in any language were what they were most afraid of and in English it was the body, that was even scarier than God. You could also say Jeesus Christ, but it meant you were angry or disgusted. I learned about religion the way most children then learned about sex, not in the gutter but in the gravel and cement schoolyard, during the winter months of real school. They would cluster in groups, holding each others' mittened hands and whispering. They terrified me by telling me there was a dead man in the sky watching everything I did and I retaliated by explaining where babies came from. Some of their mothers phoned mine to complain, though I think I was more upset than they were: they didn't believe me but I believed them.

I finish the toast; the bacon is done too, I dish it out, pouring the fat afterwards into the fire, keeping my hand back from the spurt of flame.

After breakfast David says "What's on the agenda?" I tell them I would like to search the trail that runs for half a mile close to the shore; my father may have gone along it to get wood. There was another trail that went back almost as far as the swamp but it was my brother's and secret, by now it must be illegible.

He can't have left the island, both canoes are in the toolshed and the aluminum motorboat is padlocked to a tree near the dock; the gas tanks for the motor are empty.

"Anyway," I say, "there's only two places he can be, on the island or in the lake." My head contradicts me: someone could have picked him up here and taken him to the village at the other end of the lake, it would be the perfect way to vanish; maybe he wasn't here during the winter at all.

But that's avoiding, it's not unusual for a man to disappear in the bush, it happens dozens of times each year. All it takes is a small mistake, going too far from the house in winter, blizzards are sudden, or twisting your leg so you can't walk out, in spring the blackflies would finish you, they crawl inside your clothes, you'd be covered with blood and delirious in a day. I can't accept it though, he knew too much, he was too careful.

I give David the machete, I don't know what shape the trail will be in, we may have to brush it out; Joe carries the hatchet. Before we start I coat their wrists and ankles with bug spray, and my own also. I used to be immune to mosquitoes, I'd been bitten so much, but I've lost it: on my legs and body are several itchy pink bumps from last night. The sound of love in the north, a kiss, a slap.

It's overcast, lowhanging cloud; there's a slight wind from the southeast, it may rain later or it may miss us, the weather here comes in pockets, like oil. We go in through the neck-high grass mixed with wild raspberry canes between the garden and the lake, past the burn heap and the compost heap. I should have unearthed the garbage, to see how recent it is; there's a pit also, where the burned tin cans are smashed flat and buried, that could be excavated. My father viewed as an archeological problem.

We're on the trail inside the forest; the first part is fairly open, though now and then we pass gigantic stumps, level and saw-cut, remnants of the trees that were here before the district was logged out. The trees will never be allowed to grow that tall again, they're killed as soon as they're valuable, big trees are scarce as whales.

The forest thickens and I watch for the blazes, still visible after fourteen years; the trees they're cut on have grown swollen edges around the wounds, scar tissue.

We begin to climb and my husband catches up with me again, making one of the brief appearances, framed memories he specializes in: crystal clear image enclosed by a blank wall. He's writing his own initials on a fence, graceful scrolls to show me how, lettering was one of the things he taught. There are other initials on the fence but he's making his bigger, leaving his mark. I can't identify the date or place, it was a city, before we were married; I lean beside him, admiring the fall of winter sunlight over his cheekbone and the engraved nose, noble and sloped like a Roman coin profile; that was when everything he did was perfect. On his hand is a leather glove. He said he loved me, the magic word, it was supposed to make everything light up, I'll never trust that word again.

My bitterness about him surprises me: I was what's known as the offending party, the one who left, he didn't do anything to me. He wanted a child, that's normal, he wanted us to be married.

In the morning while we were doing the dishes I decided to ask Anna. She was wiping a plate, humming snatches of The Big Rock Candy Mountain under her breath. "How do you manage it?" I said.

She stopped humming. "Manage what?"

"Being married. How do you keep it together?"

She glanced at me quickly as though she was suspicious. "We tell a lot of jokes."

"No but really," I said. If there was a secret trick I wanted to learn it.

She talked to me then, or not to me exactly but to an invisible microphone suspended above her head: people's voices go radio when they give advice. She said you just had to make an emotional commitment, it was like skiing, you couldn't see in advance what would happen but you had to let go. Let go of what, I wanted to ask her; I was measuring myself against what she was saying. Maybe that was why I failed, because I didn't know what I had to let go of. For me it hadn't been like skiing, it was more like jumping off a cliff.

That was the feeling I had all the time I was married; in the air, going down, waiting for the smash at the bottom.

"How come it didn't work out, with you?" Anna said.

"I don't know," I said, "I guess I was too young."

She nodded sympathetically. "You're lucky you didn't have kids though."

"Yes," I said. She doesn't have any herself; if she did she couldn't have said that to me. I've never told her about the baby; I haven't told Joe either, there's no reason to. He won't find out the usual way, there aren't any pictures of it peering out from a crib or a window or through the bars of a playpen in my bureau drawer or my billfold where he could stumble across them and act astonished or outraged or sad. I have to behave as though it doesn't exist, because for me it can't, it was taken away from me, exported, deported. A section of my own life, sliced off from me like a Siamese twin, my own flesh cancelled. Lapse, relapse, I have to forget.

The trail's winding now through high ground where there are boulders coming up out of the earth, carried and dropped by glaciers, moss on them and ferns, it's a damp climate. I keep my eyes on the ground, names reappearing, wintergreen, wild mint, Indian cucumber; at one time I could list every plant here that could be used or eaten. I memorized survival manuals, *How To Stay Alive in the Bush, Animal Tracks and Signs, The Woods in Winter,* at the age when the ones in the city were reading True Romance magazines: it wasn't till then I realized it was in fact possible to lose your way. Maxims float up: always carry matches and you will not starve, in a snowstorm dig a hole, avoid unclassified mushrooms, your hands and feet are the most important, if they freeze you're finished. Worthless knowledge; the pulp magazines with their cautionary tales, maidens who give in and get punished with mongoloid infants, fractured spines, dead mothers or men stolen by their best friends would have been more practical.

The trail dips down and across a swamp inlet at the tip of a bay, cedars here and bullrushes, blueflags, ooze. I go slowly, looking for footprints. There's nothing but a deer track, no sign of anyone: apparently Paul and the searchers didn't make it this far. The mosquitoes have scented us and swarm around our heads; Joe swears gently, David loudly, at the end of the line I hear Anna slapping.

We swing away from the shore and here it's a jungle, branches growing in across the path, hazel and moose maple, pithy junk trees. Sight is blocked two feet in, trunks and leaves a solid interlocking fence, green, green-grey, greybrown. None of the branches is chopped or broken back, if he's been here he's gone miraculously around and between them rather than through. I stand aside and David hacks at the wall with his machete, not very well; he tatters and bends rather than slicing.

We come up against a tree fallen across the trail. It's brought several young balsams down with it: they lie tangled together, logjam. "I don't think anyone's been through here," I say, and Joe says "Right on," he's annoyed: it's obvious. I peer into the forest to see if another trail has been cut around the windfall but there's no sign; or there are too many signs, since I'm anxious every opening between two trees looks like a path.

David prods at the dead trunk with the machete, poking holes in the bark. Joe sits down on the ground: he's breathing hard, too much city, and the flies are getting to him, he scratches his neck and the backs of his hands. "I guess that's it," I say because I have to be the one to confess defeat, and Anna says "Thank god, they're eating me alive."

We start back. He could still be in there somewhere but I seen now the impossibility of searching the island for him, it's two miles long. It would take twenty or thirty men at least, strung out at intervals and walking straight through the forest, and even then they could miss him, dead or alive, accident or suicide or murder. Or if for some unfathomable reason he's chosen this absence and is hiding, they'd never find him: there would be nothing easier in this country than to let the searchers get ahead of you and then follow at a distance, stopping when they stop, keeping them in sight so that no matter which way they turned you would always be behind them. That's what I would do.

We walk through the green light, feet muffled on wet decaying leaves. The trail is altered going back: I'm at the end now. Every few steps I glance to each side, eyes straining, scanning the ground for evidence, for anything human: a button, a cartridge, a discarded bit of paper.

It's like the times he used to play hide and seek with us in the semi-dark after supper, it was different from playing in a house, the space to hide in was endless; even when we knew which tree he had gone behind there was the fear that what would come out when you called would be someone else.

Chapter Six

No one can expect anything else from me. I checked everything, I tried; now I'm absolved from knowing. I should be
telling someone official, filling in forms, getting help as you're
supposed to in an emergency. But it's like searching for a ring
lost on a beach or in the snow: futile. There's no act I can
perform except waiting; tomorrow Evans will ship us to the
village, and after that we'll travel to the city and the present
tense. I've finished what I came for and I don't want to stay
here, I want to go back to where there is electricity and dis-
traction. I'm used to it now, filling the time without it is an
effort.

The others are trying to amuse themselves. Joe and David
are out in one of the canoes; I should have made them take
life-jackets, neither of them can steer, they're shifting their
paddles from side to side. I can see them from the front
window and from the side window I can see Anna, partly
hidden by trees. She's lying on her belly in bikini and sun-
glasses, reading a murder mystery, though she must be cold:
the sky has cleared a little, but when the clouds move in front
of the sun the heat shuts off.

Except for the bikini and the colour of her hair she could
be me at sixteen, sulking on the dock, resentful at being away
from the city and the boyfriend I'd proved my normality by

obtaining; I wore his ring, too big for any of my fingers, around my neck on a chain, like a crucifix or a military decoration. Joe and David, when distance has disguised their faces and their awkwardness, might be my brother and my father. The only place left for me is that of my mother; a problem, what she did in the afternoons between the routines of lunch and supper. Sometimes she would take breadcrumbs or seeds out to the bird feeder tray and wait for the jays, standing quiet as a tree, or she would pull weeds in the garden; but on some days she would simply vanish, walk off by herself into the forest. Impossible to be like my mother, it would need a time warp; she was either ten thousand years behind the rest or fifty years ahead of them.

I brush my hair in front of the mirror, delaying; then I turn back to my work, my deadline, the career I suddenly found myself having, I didn't intend to but I had to find something I could sell. I'm still awkward with it, I don't know what clothes to wear to interviews: it feels strapped to me, like an aqualung or an extra, artificial limb. I have a title though, a classification, and that helps: I'm what they call a commercial artist, or, when the job is more pretentious, an illustrator. I do posters, covers, a little advertising and magazine work and the occasional commissioned book like this one. For a while I was going to be a real artist; he thought that was cute but misguided, he said I should study something I'd be able to use because there have never been any important woman artists. That was before we were married and I still listened to what he said, so I went into Design and did fabric patterns. But he was right, there never have been any.

This is the fifth book I've done; the first was a Department of Manpower employment manual, young people with lobotomized grins, rapturous in their padded slots: Computer Programmer, Welder, Executive Secretary, Lab Technician. Line drawings and a few graphs. The others were children's books and so is this one, *Quebec Folk Tales*, it's a translation. It isn't my territory but I need the money. I've had the typescript three weeks, I haven't come up with any final illustrations yet. As a rule I work faster than that.

The stories aren't what I expected; they're like German fairy tales, except for the absence of red-hot iron slippers and nail-studded casks. I wonder if this mercy descends from the original tellers, from the translator or from the publisher; probably it's Mr. Percival the publisher, he's a cautious man, he shies away from anything he calls "disturbing." We had an argument about that: he said one of my drawings was too frightening and I said children liked being frightened. "It isn't the children who buy the books," he said, "it's their parents." So I compromised; now I compromise before I take the work in, it saves time. I've learned the sort of thing he wants: elegant and stylized, decoratively coloured, like patisserie cakes. I can do that, I can imitate anything: fake Walt Disney, Victorian etchings in sepia, Bavarian cookies, ersatz Eskimo for the home market. Though what they like best is something they hope will interest the English and American publishers too.

Clean water in a glass, brushes in another glass, watercolours and acrylics in their metal toothpaste tubes. Bluebottle fly near my elbow, metallic abdomen gleaming, sucker tongue walking on the oilcloth like a seventh foot. When it was raining we would sit at this table and draw in our scrapbooks with crayons or coloured pencils, anything we liked. In school you had to do what the rest were doing.

> On the crest of the hill for all to see
> God planted a Scarlet Maple Tree

printed thirty-five times, strung out along the top of the blackboard, each page with a preserved maple leaf glued to it, ironed between sheets of wax paper.

I outline a princess, an ordinary one, emaciated fashion-model torso and infantile face, like those I did for *Favourite Fairy Tales*. Earlier they annoyed me, the stories never revealed the essential things about them, such as what they ate

47

or whether their towers and dungeons had bathrooms, it was as though their bodies were pure air. It wasn't Peter Pan's ability to fly that made him incredible for me, it was the lack of an outhouse near his underground burrow.

My princess tilts her head: she's gazing up at a bird rising from a nest of flames, wings outspread like a heraldic emblem or a fire insurance trademark: The Tale of the Golden Phoenix. The bird has to be yellow and the fire can only be yellow too, they have to keep the cost down so I can't use red; that way I lose orange and purple also. I asked for red instead of yellow but Mr. Percival wanted "a cool tone."

I pause to judge: the princess looks stupified rather than filled with wonder. I discard her and try again, but this time she's crosseyed and has one breast bigger than the other. My fingers are stiff, maybe I'm getting arthritis.

I skim the story again for a different episode, but no pictures form. It's hard to believe that anyone here, even the grandmothers, ever knew these stories: this isn't a country of princesses, The Fountain of Youth and The Castle of the Seven Splendours don't belong here. They must have told stories about something as they sat around the kitchen range at night: bewitched dogs and malevolent trees perhaps, and the magic powers of rival political candidates, whose effigies in straw they burned during elections.

But the truth is that I don't know what the villagers thought or talked about, I was so shut off from them. The older ones occasionally crossed themselves when we passed, possibly because my mother was wearing slacks, but even that was never explained. Although we played during visits with the solemn, slightly hostile children of Paul and Madame, the games were brief and wordless. We never could find out what went on inside the tiny hillside church they filed into on Sundays: our parents wouldn't let us sneak up and peer through the windows, which made it illicit and attractive. After my brother began going to school in the winters he told me it was called the Mass and what they did inside was eat;

I imagined it as a sort of birthday party, with ice cream – birthday parties were my only experience then of people eating in groups – but according to my brother all they had was soda crackers.

When I started school myself I begged to be allowed to go to Sunday School, like everyone else; I wanted to find out, also I wanted to be less conspicuous. My father didn't approve, he reacted as though I'd asked to go to a pool hall: Christianity was something he'd escaped from, he wished to protect us from its distortions. But after a couple of years he decided I was old enough, I could see for myself, reason would defend me.

I knew what you wore, itchy white stockings and a hat and gloves; I went with one of the girls from school whose family took a pursed-mouth missionary interest in me. It was a United Church, it stood on a long grey street of block-shaped buildings. On the steeple instead of a cross there was a thing like an onion going around which they said was a ventilator, and inside it smelled of face powder and damp wool trousers. The Sunday School part was in the cellar; it had blackboards like a regular school, with KICKAPOO JOY JUICE printed on one of them in orange chalk and underneath, in green chalk, the mysterious initials C.G.I.T. This was a possible clue, until they translated it for me, Canadian Girls In Training. The teacher wore maroon nail-polish and a blue pancake-sized hat clipped to her head by two prongs; she told us a lot about her admirers and their cars. At the end she handed out pictures of Jesus, who didn't have thorns and ribs but was alive and draped in a bed sheet, tired-looking, surely incapable of miracles.

After church every time, the family I went with drove to a hill above the railway terminal to watch the trains shunting back and forth; it was their Sunday treat. Then they would have me to lunch, which was always the same thing, pork and beans and canned pineapple for dessert. At the beginning the father would say Grace, "For what we are about to receive may

49

the Lord make us truly thankful, Amen," while the four children pinched and kicked each other under the table; and at the end he would say,

> Pork and beans the musical fruit,
> The more you eat the more you toot.

The mother, who had a bun of greying hair and prickles around her mouth like a schmoo, would frown and ask me what I'd learned about Jesus that morning, and the father would grin feebly, ignored by all; he was a clerk in a bank, the Sunday trains his only diversion, the little rhyme his only impropriety. For some time I had a confused notion that canned pineapple really was musical and would make you sing better, until my brother set me straight.

"Maybe I'll be a Catholic," I said to my brother; I was afraid to say it to my parents.

"Catholics are crazy," he said. The Catholics went to a school down the street from ours and the boys threw snowballs at them in winter and rocks in spring and fall. "They believe in the B.V.M."

I didn't know what that was and neither did he, so he said "They believe if you don't go to Mass you'll turn into a wolf."

"Will you?" I said.

"We don't go," he said, "and we haven't."

Maybe that's why they didn't waste any sweat searching for my father, they were afraid to, they thought he'd turned into a wolf; he'd be a prime candidate since he never went to Mass at all. *Les maudits anglais,* the damned English, they mean it; they're sure we're all damned literally. There should be a *loup-garou* story in *Quebec Folk Tales,* perhaps there was and Mr. Percival took it out, it was too rough for him. But in some of the stories they do it the other way round, the animals are human inside and they take their fur skins off as easily as getting undressed.

I remember the hair on Joe's back, vestigial, like appendices and little toes: soon we'll evolve into total baldness. I like the hair though, and the heavy teeth, thick shoulders, unexpectedly slight hips, hands whose texture I can still feel on my skin, roughened and leathery from the clay. Everything I value about him seems to be physical: the rest is either unknown, disagreeable or ridiculous. I don't care much for his temperament, which alternates between surliness and gloom, or for the overgrown pots he throws so skilfully on the wheel and then multilates, cutting holes in them, strangling them, slashing them open. That's unfair, he never uses a knife, only his fingers, and a lot of the time he only bends them, doubles them over; even so they have a disagreeable mutant quality. Nobody else admires them either: the aspiring housewives he teaches two evenings a week, Pottery and Ceramics 432-A, want to make ashtrays and plates with cheerful daisies on them instead, and the things don't sell at all in the few handicraft shops that will even stock them. So they accumulate in our already cluttered basement apartment like fragmentary memories or murder victims. I can't even put flowers in them, the water would run out through the rips. Their only function is to uphold Joe's unvoiced claim to superior artistic seriousness: every time I sell a poster design or get a new commission he mangles another pot.

I wanted my third princess to be running lightly through a meadow but the paper's too wet, she gets out of control, sprouting an enormous rear; I try to salvage it by turning it into a bustle, but it's not convincing. I give up and doodle, adding fangs and a moustache, surrounding her with moons and fish and a wolf with bristling hackles and a snarl; but that doesn't work either, it's more like an overweight collie. What's the alternative to princesses, what else will parents buy for their children? Humanoid bears and talking pigs, Protestant choo-choo trains who make the grade and become successful.

Perhaps it's not only his body I like, perhaps it's his failure; that also has a kind of purity.

I crumple up my third princess, dump the paint water into the slop pail and clean the brushes. I survey from the windows:

David and Joe are still out on the lake but they seem to be heading back now. Anna is halfway up the hillside stairs, towel over her arm. I see her for a moment faceted by the screen door and then she's inside.

"Hi," she says, "get anything done?"

"Not much," I say.

She comes over to the table and smooths out my botched princesses. "That's good," she says without conviction.

"Those are mistakes," I say.

"Oh." She turns the sheets over, face down. "Did you believe that stuff when you were little?" she says. "I did, I thought I was really a princess and I'd end up living in a castle. They shouldn't let kids have stuff like that." She goes to the mirror, blots and smooths her face, then stands on tiptoe, checking her back to see if it's pink. "What was he *doing* up here?" she asks suddenly.

It takes me a moment to understand what she means. My father, his work. "I don't know," I say. "Just, you know."

She gives me an odd glance, as though I've violated a propriety, and I'm puzzled, she told me once you shouldn't define yourself by your job but by who you are. When they ask her what she does she talks about fluidity and Being rather than Doing; though if she doesn't like the person she just says "I'm David's wife."

"He was living," I say. This is almost right, it satisfies her, she goes into the bedroom to change her clothes.

All at once I'm furious with him for vanishing like this, unresolved, leaving me with no answers to give them when they ask. If he was going to die he should have done it visibly, out in the open, so they could mark him with a stone and get it over with.

They must find it strange, a man his age staying alone the whole winter in a cabin ten miles from nowhere; I never questioned it, to me it was logical. They always intended to move here permanently as soon as they could, when he retired: isolation was to him desirable. He didn't dislike people,

52

he merely found them irrational; animals, he said, were more consistent, their behaviour at least was predictable. To him that's what Hitler exemplified: not the triumph of evil but the failure of reason. He found war irrational too, both of my parents were pacifists, but he would have fought anyway, in defence of science perhaps, if he'd been permitted; this must be the only country where a botanist can be classified as crucial to the national defense.

As it was he withdrew; we could have lived all year in the company town but he split us between two anonymities, the city and the bush. In the city we lived in a succession of apartments and in the bush he picked the most remote lake he could find, when my brother was born there wasn't yet a road to it. Even the village had too many people for him, he needed an island, a place where he could recreate not the settled farm life of his own father but that of the earliest ones who arrived when there was nothing but forest and no ideologies but the ones they brought with them. When they say Freedom they never quite mean it, what they mean is freedom from interference.

The stack of papers is still up on the shelf by the lamp. I've been avoiding it, looking through it would be an intrusion if he were still alive. But now I've admitted he's dead I might as well find out what he left for me. Executor.

I was expecting a report of some kind, tree growth or diseases, unfinished business; but on the top page there's only a crude drawing of a hand, done with a felt pen or a brush, and some notations: numbers, a name. I flip through the next few pages. More hands, then a stiff childish figure, faceless and minus the hands and feet, and on the next page a similar creature with two things like tree branches or antlers protruding from its head. On each of the pages are the numbers, and on some a few scrawled words: LICHENS RED CLOTHING LEFT. I can't make sense out of them. The handwriting is my father's, but changed, more hasty or careless.

Outside I hear the crunch of wood on wood as the canoe

hits the dock, they've brought it in too fast; then their laughter. I reach the stack of papers back to the shelf, I don't want them to see.

That's what he was doing here all winter, he was shut up in this cabin making these unintelligible drawings. I sit at the table, my heart speeded up as if I've opened what I thought was an empty closet and found myself face to face with a thing that isn't supposed to be there, like a claw or a bone. This is the forgotten possibility: he might have gone insane. Crazy, loony. Bushed, the trappers call it when you stay in the forest by yourself too long. And if insane, perhaps not dead: none of the rules would be the same.

Anna walks out of the bedroom, dressed in jeans and shirt again. She combs her hair in front of the mirror, light ends, dark roots, humming to herself, You Are My Sunshine; smoke twines up from her cigarette. *Help*, I think at her silently, *talk*. And she does.

"What's for dinner?" she says; then, waving, "Here they come."

Chapter Seven

At supper we finish off the beer. David wants to go fishing, it's the last night, so I leave the dishes for Anna and go down to the garden with the shovel and the tin can saved from the peas.

I dig in the weediest part near the compost heap, lifting the earth and letting it crumble, sieving the worms out with my fingers. The soil is rich, the worms scramble, red ones and pink ones.

> Nobody loves me
> Everybody hates me
> I'm going to the garden to eat worms.

They sang that back and forth at recess: it was an insult, but perhaps they are edible. They're sold like apples in season, VERS 5¢ on the roadside signs, sometimes VERS 5¢, later VERS 10¢, inflation. French class, *vers libre*, I translated it the first time as Free Worms and she thought I was being smart.

I put the worms in the can and some dirt for them. As I walk back to the cabin I hold my palm over the top; already they're nudging with their head ends, trying to get out. I make them a cover from a piece of paper torn off the grocery bag, keeping it on with a rubber band. My mother was a saver:

rubber bands, string, safety pins, jam jars, for her the Depression never ended.

David is fitting the sections of his borrowed fishing rod together; it's fibreglass, I have no faith in it. I take the steel trolling rod from its hooks on the wall. "Come on," I tell David, "you can use that one for still-fishing."

"Show me how to light the lamp," Anna says, "I'll stay here and read."

I don't want to leave her alone. What I'm afraid of is my father, hidden on the island somewhere and attracted by the light perhaps, looming up at the window like a huge ragged moth; or, if he's still at all lucid, asking her who she is and ordering her out of his house. As long as there are four of us he'll keep away, he never liked groups.

"Poor sport," David says.

I tell her I need her in the canoe for extra weight, which is a lie as we'll be too heavy already, but she takes my expert word.

While they're getting into the canoe I return to the garden and catch a small leopard frog as an emergency weapon. I put it in a jam jar and punch a few airholes in the lid.

Tackle box, smelling of stale fish, old captures; worm can and frog bottle, knife and heap of bracken fronds for the fish to bleed on. Joe in the bow, Anna behind him on a life-jacket facing me, David on another life-jacket with his back to me and his legs tangled in amongst Anna's. Before I push off I clip a silver and gold spinner with glass ruby eyes to David's line and hook a worm on, looping its body seductively. Both ends twirl.

"Ech," says Anna, who can see what I'm doing.

"It doesn't hurt them," my brother said, "they don't feel it." "Then why do they squirm?" I said. He said it was nervous tension.

"Whatever happens," I tell them, "stay in the middle." We move ponderously out of the bay. I've taken on too much: I haven't been in a canoe for years, my muscles are shot, Joe paddles as though he's stirring the lake with a ladle and we're down by the bow. But none of them will know the difference. I think, it's a good thing our lives don't depend on catching a fish. Starvation, bite your arm and suck the blood, that's what they do on lifeboats; or the Indian way, if there's no bait try a chunk of your flesh.

The island shoreline recedes behind us, he can't follow us here. Above the trees streaky mackerel clouds are spreading in over the sky, paint on a wet page; no wind at lake level, soft feel of the air before rain. The fish like this, the mosquitoes too, but I can't use any bug spray because it would get on the bait and the fish would smell it.

I steer us along the mainland shore. A blue heron lifts from a bay where it's been fishing and flaps overhead, neck and beak craning forward and long legs stretched back, winged snake. It notes us with a rasping pterodactyl croak and rises higher, heading southeast, there was a colony of them, it must still be there. But now I have to pay more attention to David. The copper line slants down, cutting the water, vibrating slightly.

"Any action?" I ask.

"It's just sort of jigging."

"That's the spoon turning," I say. "Keep the tip down; if you feel a nibble wait a second and then give it a sharp tug, okay?"

"Right," he says.

My arms are tired. Behind me I can hear the tick tock of the frog hopping up and hitting its muzzle against the jar lid.

When we're getting near the sheer cliff I tell him to reel in, we'll still-fish and he can use his own rod.

"Lie down, Anna," he says, "I'm gonna use my own rod."

Anna says "Oh Christ, you have to do that about everything, don't you?"

He chuckles at her and reels and the line comes in, the water slipping off it; the pale gleam of the spoon wavers up out of the lake. When it skips over the surface towards us I can see the worm is gone. On one hook is a shred of worm skin; I used to wonder how the lures with their crude African-idol eyes could deceive the fish, but perhaps they've learned.

We're opposite the cliff, grey slab of rock straight as a monument, overhanging slightly, ledge like a step halfway up, brown rock-lichen growing in the fissures. I put a lead sinker and a different spoon and a fresh worm on David's line and toss it over; the worm drops, pink, pink-brown, till it disappears in the shadow of the cliff. The dark torpedo shapes of the fish are seeing it, sniffing at it, prodding it with their noses. I believe in them the way other people believe in God: I can't see them but I know they are there.

"Keep right still," I say to Anna, who's beginning to shift uncomfortably. They can hear.

Light fading, silence; back in the forest, liquid spiral thrush voice, they call at sunset. David's arm moves up and down.

When nothing happens I tell him to reel in; the worm is gone again. I take out the little frog, the ultimate solution, and hook it on securely while it squeaks. Other people always did that for me.

"God you're cold-blooded," Anna says. The frog goes down through the water, kicking like a man swimming.

Everyone concentrates, even Anna: they sense this is my last trick. I stare into the water, it was always a kind of meditation. My brother fished by technique, he outguessed them, but I fished by prayer, listening.

> Our father who art in heaven
> Please let the fish be caught.

Later when I knew that wouldn't work, just *Please be caught*, invocation or hypnosis. He got more fish but I could pretend mine were willing, they had chosen to die and forgiven me in advance.

I begin to think the frog has failed. But it's still magic, the rod bends like a diviner's and Anna shrieks with surprise.

I say "Keep the line tight," but David is oblivious, he's reeling like a mixmaster and saying "Wow, wow" to himself and it's up to the surface, it jumps clear and hangs in the air like a framed photo over a bar only moving. It dives and pulls, the line slackens, it's doubling back trying to shake loose; but when it jumps again David jerks the rod with his whole body and it sails across and flops into the canoe, a dumb move, he could've lost it, on top of Anna and she lurches, screaming "Get it off me! Get it off me!" and we almost tip. Joe says "Holy shit" and grabs at the side, I bend the other way, counterbalancing, David is snatching at it. It slithers over the canoe ribs, flippering and snapping.

"Here," I say, "hit it back of the eyes." I reach him the sheathed knife, I'd rather not kill it myself.

David swipes at it, misses; Anna cover her eyes and says "Ugh. Ugh." It flops towards me and I step down on it with my foot and grab the knife and whack it quickly with the knife handle, crushing the skull, and it trembles stiffly all over, that's done it.

"What is it?" David asks, amazed by what he's caught but proud too. They are all laughing, joyful with victory and relief, like the newsreels of parades at the end of the war, and that makes me glad. Their voices bounce off the cliff.

"Walleye," I say, "Pickerel. We'll have it for breakfast."

It's a good size. I pick it up, fingers hooked under the gills and holding firmly, they can bite and jerk loose even when they're dead. I put it on the bracken fronds and rinse my hand and the knife. One of its eyes is bulging out and I feel a little sick, it's because I've killed something, made it dead; but I know that's irrational, killing certain things is all right, food and enemies, fish and mosquitoes; and wasps, when there are too many of them you pour boiling water down their tunnels. "Don't bother them and they won't bother you," our mother would say when they lit on our plates. That was before the house was built, we were living outside in tents. Our father said they went in cycles.

"Neat eh?" David says to the others; he's excited, he wants praise. "Ugh," says Anna, "it's slimy, I'm not going to eat any of it." Joe grunts, I wonder if he's jealous.

David wants to try for another; it's like gambling, you only stop if you lose. I don't remind him I have no more magic frogs; I get out a worm for him and let him hook it on himself.

He fishes for a while but he's having no luck. Just as Anna's beginning to fidget again I hear a whine, motorboat. I listen, it may be going somewhere else, but it rounds a point and becomes a roar, homing in on us, big powerboat, the white water veeing from the bow. The engine cuts and it skids in beside us, its wash rocking us sharply. American flag on the front and another at the back, two irritated-looking businessmen with pug-dog faces and nifty outfits and a thin shabby man from the village, guiding. I see it's Claude from the motel, he scowls at us, he feels we're poaching on his preserve.

"Getting any?" one of the Americans yells, teeth bared, friendly as a shark.

I say "No" and nudge David with my foot. He'd want to tell, if only to spite them.

The other American throws his cigar butt over the side. "This don't look like much of a place," he says to Claude.

"Used to be," Claude says.

"Next year I'm goin' to Florida," the first American says.

"Reel in," I say to David. There's no sense in staying here now. If they catch one they'll be here all night, if they don't get anything in fifteen minutes they'll blast off and scream around the lake in their souped-up boat, deafening the fish. They're the kind who catch more than they can eat and they'd do it with dynamite if they could get away with it.

We used to think they were harmless and funny and inept and faintly lovable, like President Eisenhower. We met two of them once on the way to the bass lake, they were carrying their tin motorboat and the motor over the portage so they wouldn't have to paddle once they were on the inner lake; when we first heard them thrashing along through the underbrush we thought they were bears. Another one turned up with a spinning reel and stepped in our campfire, scorching his new boots; when he tried to cast he sent his plug, a real minnow sealed in transparent plastic, into the bushes on the other side of the bay. We laughed at him behind his back and asked if he was catching squirrels but he didn't mind, he showed us his automatic firelighter and his cook set with detachable handles and his collapsible armchair. They liked everything collapsible.

On the way back we hug the shore, avoiding the open lake in case the Americans take it into their heads to zoom past us as close as possible, they sometimes do that for fun, their wake could tip us. But before we're half the distance they whoosh away into nowhere like Martians in a late movie, and I relax.

When we get back I'll hang up the fish and wash the scales and the salty armpit odour off my hands with soap. After that I'll light the lamp and the fire and make some cocoa. Being here feels right to me for the first time, and I know it's because we're leaving tomorrow. My father will have the island to himself; madness is private, I respect that, however he may be living it's better than an institution. Before we go I'll burn his drawings, they're evidence of the wrong sort.

The sun has set, we slide back through the gradual dusk. Loon voices in the distance; bats flitter past us, dipping over the watersurface, flat calm now, the shore things, white-grey rocks and dead trees, doubling themselves in the dark mirror. Around us the illusion of infinite space or of no space, ourselves and the obscure shore which it seems we could touch, the water between an absence. The canoe's reflection floats with us, the paddles twin in the lake. It's like moving on air, nothing beneath us holding us up; suspended, we drift home.

Chapter Eight

In the early morning Joe wakes me; his hands at any rate are intelligent, they move over me delicately as a blind man's reading braille, skilled, moulding me like a vase, they're learning me; they repeat patterns he's tried before, they've found out what works, and my body responds that way too, anticipates him, educated, crisp as a typewriter. It's best when you don't know them. A phrase comes to me, a joke then but mournful now, someone in a parked car after a highschool dance who said *With a paper bag over their head they're all the same.* At the time I didn't understand what he meant, but since then I've pondered it. It's almost like a coat of arms: two people making love with paper bags over their heads, not even any eyeholes. Would that be good or bad?

When we're finished and after we rest I get up and dress and go out to prepare the fish. It's been hanging all night, the string through its gills looped to a tree branch out of the reach of scavengers, racoons, otters, mink, skunks. A squeezing of fish shit, like a bird's only browner, drools from the anus. I untie the string and carry the fish down to the lake to clean and fillet it.

I kneel on the flat rock beside the lake, the knife and the plate for the fillets beside me. This was never my job; someone else did it, my brother or my father. I cut off the head and tail and slit the belly and open the fish into its two halves. Inside the stomach is a partly digested leech and some shreds of crayfish. I divide along the backbone, then along the two lateral lines: four pieces, blueish white, translucent. The entrails will be buried in the garden, they're fertilizer.

As I'm washing the fillets David saunters down to the dock with his toothbrush. "Hey," he says, "is that my fish?" He regards the guts on the plate with interest. "Hold it," he says, "that's a Random Sample." He goes for Joe and the camera and the two of them solemnly film the fish innards, collapsed bladders and tubes and soft ropes, rearranging them between takes for better angles. It would never occur to David to have someone snap him with a Brownie camera holding his fish up by the tail and grinning, nor would he ever have it stuffed and mounted; still, he wants to immortalize it, in his own way. Photo album, I'm in it somewhere, successive incarnations of me preserved and flattened like flowers pressed in dictionaries, that was the other book she kept, the leather album, a logbook like the diaries. I used to hate standing still, waiting for the click.

I dip the fillets in flour and fry them and we eat them with strips of bacon. "Good food, good meat, Good God, let's eat," David says; and later, smacking his lips, "Couldn't get this in the city."

Anna says "Sure you could, frozen. You can get anything there now."

After breakfast I go into my room and begin to pack. Through the plywood wall I hear Anna walking, pouring more coffee, the creak as David stretches out on the couch.

Perhaps I should fold up all the bedding and towels and the abandoned clothes, tie them into bundles and take them back with me. No one will be living here now and the moths and the mice will get in eventually. If he doesn't ever decide to return I suppose it belongs to me, or half to me and half to my brother; but my brother won't do anything about it, after he left he's evaded them as much as I have. He set it up better though, he simply went as far away as he could: if I stuck a knitting needle straight through the earth the point would emerge where he is now, camped in the outback, inaccessible; he probably hasn't even got my letter yet. Mineral rights, that's what he explores, for one of the big international companies, a prospector; but I can't believe in that, nothing he's done since we grew up is real to me.

"I like it here," David says. No sound from the others. "Let's stay on for a while, a week, it'd be great."

"Don't you have that seminar?" Anna says dubiously. "Man and his Electricity Environment, or something?"

"Electrifying. That's not till August."

"I don't think we should," Anna says.

"How come you never want us to do anything I want to do?" David says, and there's a pause. Then he says "What d'you think?" and Joe says "Okay by me."

"Great," says David, "we'll do some more fishing."

I sit down on the bed. They might have asked me first, it's my house. Though maybe they're waiting till I come out, they'll ask then. If I say I don't want to they can't very well stay; but what reason can I give? I can't tell them about my father, betray him; anyway they might think I was making it up. There's my work, but they know I have it with me. I could leave by myself with Evans but I'd only get as far as the village: it's David's car, I'd have to steal the keys, and also, I remind myself, I never learned to drive.

Anna makes a last feeble attempt. "I'll run out of cigarettes."

"Do you good," David says cheerfully, "filthy habit. Get you back into shape." He's older than we are, he's over thirty, he's beginning to worry about that; every now and then he hits himself in the stomach and says "Flab."

"I'll get crabby," Anna says, but David only laughs and says "Try it."

I could tell them there isn't enough food. But they'd spot that as a lie, there's the garden and the rows of cans on the shelves, corned beef, Spam, baked beans, chicken, powdered milk, everything.

I go to the room door, open it. "You'll have to pay Evans the five anyway," I say.

For a moment they're startled, they realize I've overheard. Then David says "No sweat." He gives me a quick look, triumphant and appraising, as though he's just won something: not a war but a lottery.

When Evans turns up at the appointed time David and Joe go down to the dock to arrange things with him. I warned them not to say anything about the fish: if they do, this part of the lake will be swarming with Americans, they have an uncanny way of passing the word, like ants about sugar, or lobsters. After a few minutes I hear the boat starting again and accelerating and diminishing, he's gone.

I've avoided Evans and the explanation and negotiations by going up to the outhouse and latching myself in. That was where I went when there was something I didn't want to do, like weeding the garden. It's the new outhouse, the old one got used up. This one is built of logs; my brother and I made the hole for it, he dug with the shovel and I hauled the sand up in a pail. Once a porcupine fell in, they like to chew axe handles and toilet seats.

In the city I never hid in bathrooms; I didn't like them, they were too hard and white. The only city place I can remember hiding is behind opened doors at birthday parties. I despised them, the pew-purple velvet dresses with anti-macassar lace collars and the presents, voices going Oooo with envy when they were opened, and the pointless games, finding a thimble or memorizing clutter on a tray. There were only two things you could be, a winner or a loser; the mothers tried to rig it so everyone got a prize, but they couldn't figure out what to do about me since I wouldn't play. At first I ran away, but after that my mother said I had to go, I had to learn to be polite; "civilized," she called it. So I watched from behind the door. When I finally joined in a game of Musical Chairs I was welcomed with triumph, like a religious convert or a political defector.

Some were disappointed, they found my hermit-crab habits amusing, they found me amusing in general. Each year it was a different school, in October or November when the first snow hit the lake, and I was the one who didn't know the local customs, like a person from another culture: on me they could try out the tricks and minor tortures they'd already used up on each other. When the boys chased and captured the girls after school and tied them up with their own skipping ropes, I was the one they would forget on purpose to untie. I spent many afternoons looped to fences and gates and convenient trees, waiting for a benevolent adult to pass and free me; later I became an escape artist of sorts, expert at undoing knots. On better days they would gather around, competing for me.

"Adam and Eve and Pinch Me," they shouted,

> Went to the river to bathe;
> Adam and Eve fell in,
> So who do you think was saved?

"I don't know," I said.

"You have to answer," they said, "that's the rules."

"Adam and Eve," I said craftily. "*They* were saved."

"If you don't do it right we won't play with you," they said. Being socially retarded is like being mentally retarded, it arouses in others disgust and pity and the desire to torment and reform.

It was harder for my brother; our mother had taught him that fighting was wrong so he came home every day beaten to a pulp. Finally she had to back down: he could fight, but only if they hit first.

I didn't last long at Sunday School. One girl told me she had prayed for a Barbara Ann Scott doll with figure skates and swansdown trim on the costume and she got it for her birthday; so I decided to pray too, not like the Lord's Prayer or the fish prayer but for something real. I prayed to be made invisible, and when in the morning everyone could still see me I knew they had the wrong God.

A mosquito lights on my arm and I let it bite me, waiting till its abdomen globes with blood before I pop it with my thumb like a grape. They need the blood before they can lay their eggs. There's a breeze, filtering through the screened window; it's better here than in the city, with the exhaust-pipe fumes and the damp heat, the burnt rubber smell of the subway, the brown grease that congeals on your skin if you walk around outside. How have I been able to live so long in the city, it isn't safe. I always felt safe here, even at night.

That's a lie, my own voice says out loud. I think hard about it, considering it, and it is a lie: sometimes I was terrified, I would shine the flashlight ahead of me on the path, I would hear a rustling in the forest and know it was hunting me, a bear, a wolf or some indefinite thing with no name, that was worse.

I look around at the walls, the window; it's the same, it hasn't changed, but the shapes are inaccurate as though everything has warped slightly. I have to be more careful about my memories, I have to be sure they're my own and not the memories of other people telling me what I felt, how I acted, what I said: if the events are wrong the feelings I remember about them will be wrong too, I'll start inventing them and there will be no way of correcting it, the ones who could help are gone. I run quickly over my version of it, my life, checking it like an alibi; it fits, it's all there till the time I left. Then static, like a jumped track, for a moment I've lost it, wiped clean; my exact age even, I shut my eyes, what is it? To have the past but not the present, that means you're going senile.

I refuse to panic, I force my eyes open, my hand, life etched on it, reference: I flatten the palm and the lines fragment, spread like ripples. I concentrate on the spiderweb near the window, flyhusks caught in it catching in turn the sun, in my mouth tongue forming my name, repeating it like a chant. . . .

Then someone knocks on the door. "Ready or not, you must be caught," says a voice, it's David, I can identify him, relief, I slip back into place.

"Just a minute," I say, and he knocks again and says "Snappy with the crap in there," giving a Woody Woodpecker laugh.

Before lunch I tell them I'm going for a swim. The others don't want to, they say it will be too cold, and it is cold, like icewater. I shouldn't be going by myself, we were taught that, I might get cramps.

What I used to do was run to the end of the dock and jump, it was like a heart attack or lightning, but as I walk towards the lake I find I no longer have the nerve for that.

This was where he drowned, he got saved only by accident; if there had been a wind she wouldn't have heard him. She leaned over and reached down and grabbed him by the hair, hauled him up and poured the water out of him. His drowning never seemed to have affected him as much as I thought it should, he couldn't even remember it. If it had happened to me I would have felt there was something special about me, to be raised from the dead like that; I would have returned with secrets, I would have known things most people didn't.

After she'd told the story I asked our mother where he would have gone if she hadn't saved him. She said she didn't know. My father explained everything but my mother never did, which only convinced me that she had the answers but wouldn't tell. "Would he be in the graveyard?" I said. They had a verse about the graveyard at school too:

Stick him in the bread pan,
Sock him in the jaw;
Now he's in the graveyard,
Haw, haw haw.

"Nobody knows," she said. She was making a pie crust and she gave me a piece of the dough to distract me. My father

68

would have said Yes; he said you died when your brain died. I wonder if he still believes that.

I go off the dock and wade in from the shore, slowly, splashing water over my shoulders and neck, the cold climbing my thighs; my footsoles feel the sand and the twigs and sunk leaves. At that time I would dive and coast along the lakefloor with my eyes open, distance and my own body blurred and eroding; or out further, diving from the canoe or the raft and turning on my back under the water to look up, the bubbles fleeing from my mouth. We would stay in until our skins became numbed and turned a strange colour, bluish-purple. I must have been superhuman, I couldn't do it now. Perhaps I'm growing old, at last, can that be possible?

I stand there shivering, seeing my reflection and my feet down through it, white as fishflesh on the sand, till finally being in the air is more painful than being in the water and I bend and push myself reluctantly into the lake.

TWO

Chapter Nine

The trouble is all in the knob at the top of our bodies. I'm not against the body or the head either: only the neck, which creates the illusion that they are separate. The language is wrong, it shouldn't have different words for them. If the head extended directly into the shoulders like a worm's or a frog's without that constriction, that lie, they wouldn't be able to look down at their bodies and move them around as if they were robots or puppets; they would have to realize that if the head is detached from the body both of them will die..

I'm not sure when I began to suspect the truth, about myself and about them, what I was and what they were turning into. Part of it arrived swift as flags, as mushrooms, unfurling and sudden growth, but it was there in me, the evidence, only needing to be deciphered. From where I am now it seems as if I've always known, everything, time is compressed like the fist I close on my knee in the darkening bedroom, I hold inside it the clues and solutions and the power for what I must do now.

I was seeing poorly, translating badly, a dialect problem, I should have used my own. In the experiments they did with children, shutting them up with deaf and dumb nurses, locking them in closets, depriving them of words, they found that after a certain age the mind is incapable of absorbing any language; but how could they tell the child hadn't invented one, unrecognizable to everyone but itself? That was in the green book at high school, *Your Health*, along with the photographs of cretins and people with thyroid deficiencies, the crippled and deformed, the examples, with black oblongs across their eyes like condemned criminals: the only pictures of naked bodies it was judged proper for us to see. The rest were diagrams, transparencies with labels and arrows, the ovaries purple sea creatures, the womb a pear.

The voices of the others and the riffle and slap of cards reach me through the closed door. Canned laughter, they carry it with them, the midget reels of tape and the On switch concealed somewhere in their chests, instant playback.

After Evans left that day I was uneasy: the island wasn't safe, we were trapped on it. They didn't realize it but I did, I was responsible for them. The sense of watching eyes, his presence lurking just behind the green leafscreen, ready to pounce or take flight, he wasn't predictable, I was trying to think of ways to keep them out of danger; they would be all right as long as they didn't go anywhere alone. He might be harmless but I couldn't be sure.

We finished lunch and I took the breadcrumbs out to the tray for the birds. The jays had discovered there were people living in the cabin; they're intelligent, they knew a figure near the tray signalled food; or perhaps a few of them were old enough to remember the image of my mother, hand outstretched. Two or three of them stood sentinel now, out of reach, wary.

Joe followed me out and watched as I spread the crumbs. He put his fingers on my arm, frowning at me, which may have meant he wanted to talk to me: speech to him was a task, a battle, words mustered behind his beard and issued one at a time, heavy and square like tanks. His hand gripped me in a preliminary spasm, but David was there with the axe.

"Hey lady," he said, "I see your woodpile's gettin' low. You could use a handy man."

He wanted to do something useful; and he was right, if we were staying a week we would need a fresh supply. I asked him to find standing trees, dead but not too old or rotten, "Yes'm," he said, giving me a burlesque salute.

Joe took the small hatchet and went with him. They were from the city, I was afraid they might chop their feet; though that would be a way out, I thought, we'd have to go back. But I didn't need to warn them, about him, they had weapons. He would see that and run away.

When they'd disappeared along the trail into the forest I said I was going down to weed the garden, another job that had to be done. I wanted to keep busy, preserve at least the signs of order, conceal my fear, both from others and from him. Fear has a smell, as love does.

Anna could tell she was expected to help; she abandoned her murder mystery and stubbed out her cigarette, only half-smoked, she was rationing them. We tied scarves around our heads and I went to the toolshed for the rake.

The garden was full in sunlight and steaming hot, moist as a greenhouse. We knelt down and began to pull at the weeds; they resisted, holding on or taking clumps of soil out with them or breaking their stems, leaving their roots in the earth to regenerate; I dug for the feet in the warm dirt, my hands green with weed blood. Gradually the vegetables emerged, pallid and stunted most of them, all but strangled. We raked the weeds into piles between the rows where they wilted, dying slowly; later they would be burned, like witches, to keep them from reappearing. There were a few mosquitoes and the deer flies with their iridescent rainbow eyes and stings like heated needles.

From time to time I paused, checking the fence, the border, but no one was there. Perhaps he would be unrecognizable, his former shape transfigured by age and madness and the forest, rag bundle of decaying clothes, the skin of his face woolly with dead leaves. History, I thought, quick.

It took them years to make the garden, the real soil was too sandy and anaemic. This oblong was artificial, the product of skill and of compost spaded in, black muck dredged from swamps, horse dung ferried by boat from the winter logging camps when they still kept horses to drag the logs to the frozen lake. My father and mother would carry it in bushel baskets on the handbarrow, two poles with boards nailed across, each of them lifting an end.

I could remember before that, when we lived in tents. It was about here we found the lard pail, ripped open like a paper bag, claw scratches and toothmarks scarring the paint. Our father had gone on a long trip as he often did to investigate trees for the paper company or the government, I was never certain which he worked for. Our mother was given a three-week supply of food. The bear walked through the back of the food tent, we heard it in the night. It stepped on the eggs and tomatoes and pried open all the storage tins and scattered the wax-paper bread and smashed the jam jars, we salvaged what we could in the morning. The only thing it didn't bother with was the potatoes, and we were eating them for breakfast around the campfire when it materialized on the path, snuffling along bulky and flat-footed, an enormous fanged rug, returning for more. My mother stood up and walked towards it; it hesitated and grunted. She yelled a word at it that sounded like "Scat!" and waved her arms, and it turned around and thudded off into the forest.

That was the picture I kept, my mother seen from the back, arms upraised as though she was flying, and the bear terrified. When she told the story later she said she'd been scared to death but I couldn't believe that, she had been so positive, assured, as if she knew a foolproof magic formula: gesture and word. She was wearing her leather jacket.

"You on the pill?" Anna asked suddenly.

I looked at her, startled. It took me a minute, why did she want to know? That was what they used to call a personal question.

"Not any more," I said.

"Me neither," she said glumly. "I don't know anyone who still is any more. I got a blood clot in my leg, what did you get?" She had a smear of mud across her cheek, her pink face layer was softening in the heat, like tar.

"I couldn't see," I said. "Things were blurry. They said it would clear up after a couple of months but it didn't." It was like having vaseline on my eyes but I didn't say that.

Anna nodded; she was tugging at the weeds as though she

73

was pulling hair. "Bastards," she said, "they're so smart, you think they'd be able to come up with something that'd work without killing you. David wants me to go back on, he says it's no worse for you than aspirin, but next time it could be the heart or something. I mean, I'm not taking those kinds of chances."

Love without fear, sex without risk, that's what they wanted to be true; and they almost did it, I thought, they almost pulled it off, but as in magicians' tricks or burglaries half-success is failure and we're back to the other things. Love is taking precautions. Did you take any precautions, they say, not before but after. Sex used to smell like rubber gloves and now it does again, no more handy green plastic packages, moon-shaped so that the woman can pretend she's still natural, cyclical, instead of a chemical slot machine. But soon they'll have the artificial womb, I wonder how I feel about that. After the first I didn't ever want to have another child, it was too much to go through for nothing, they shut you into a hospital, they shave the hair off you and tie your hands down and they don't let you see, they don't want you to understand, they want you to believe it's their power, not yours. They stick needles into you so you won't hear anything, you might as well be a dead pig, your legs are up in a metal frame, they bend over you, technicians, mechanics, butchers, students clumsy or sniggering practising on your body, they take the baby out with a fork like a pickle out of a pickle jar. After that they fill your veins up with red plastic, I saw it running down through the tube. I won't let them do that to me ever again.

He wasn't there with me, I couldn't remember why; he should have been, since it was his idea, his fault. But he brought his car to collect me afterwards, I didn't have to take a taxi.

From the forest behind us came the sound of sporadic chopping: a few blows, the echoes, a pause, a few more blows, one of them laughing, echo of the laughter. It was my brother who cut the trail, the year before he left, the axe hacking and the machete slashing through the undergrowth marking his progress as he worked his way around the shore.

"Haven't we done enough?" Anna asked. "I bet I'm getting sunstroke." She sat back on her heels and took out the unsmoked half of her cigarette. I think she wanted us to exchange more confidences, she wanted to talk about her other diseases, but I kept on weeding. Potatoes, onions; the strawberry patch was a hopeless jungle, we wouldn't do that; in any case the season was over.

David and Joe appeared in the long grass outside the fence, one at either end of a thinnish log. They were proud, they'd caught something. The log was notched in many places as though they'd attacked it.

"Hi," David called. "How's the ol' plantation workers?"

Anna stood up. "Fuck off," she said, squinting at them against the sun.

"You've hardly done anything," David said, unquenchable, "you call that a garden?"

I measured their axework with my father's summarizing eye. In the city he would shake hands with them, estimating them shrewdly: could they handle an axe, what did they know about manure? They would stand there embarrassed in their washed suburban skins and highschool clothes, uncertain what was expected of them.

"That's great," I said.

David wanted us to get the movie camera and take some footage of both of them carrying the log, for *Random Samples*; he said it would be his cameo appearance. Joe said we couldn't work the camera. David said all you did was press a button, an idiot could do it, anyway it might be even better if it was out of focus or overexposed, it would introduce the element of chance, like a painter throwing paint at a canvas, it would be organic. But Joe said what if we wrecked the camera, who would pay for it. In the end they stuck the axe in the log, after several tries, and took turns shooting each other standing beside it, arms folded and one foot on it as if it was a lion or a rhinoceros.

In the evening we played bridge, with the set of slightly greasy cards that had always been there, blue seahorses on one deck, red seahorses on the other. David and Anna played against us. They won easily: Joe didn't know how, exactly, and I hadn't played for years. I was never any good; the only part I liked was picking up the cards and arranging them.

Afterwards I waited for Anna to walk up to the outhouse with me; usually I went first, alone. We took both flashlights; they made protective circles of weak yellow light, moving with our feet as they walked. Rustlings, toads in the dry leaves; once the quick warning thump of a rabbit. The sounds would be safe as long as I knew what they were.

"I wish I had a warmer sweater," Anna said, "I didn't know it got so cold."

"There's some raincoats," I said, "you could try those."

When we got back to the cabin the other two were in bed; they didn't bother going as far as the outhouse after dark, they peed on the ground. I brushed my teeth; Anna started taking off her makeup by the light of a candle and her flashlight propped on end, they'd blown out the lamp.

I went into my room and got undressed. Joe mumbled, he was half asleep; I curled my arm over him.

Outside was the wind, trees moving in it, nothing else. The yellow target from Anna's flashlight was on the ceiling; it shifted, she was going into their room and I could hear them, Anna breathing, a fast panic sound as though she was running; then her voice began, not like her real voice but twisted as her face must have been, a desperate beggar's whine, *please please*. I put the pillow over my head, I didn't want to listen, I wanted it to be through but it kept on, *Shut up* I whispered but she wouldn't. She was praying to herself, it was as if David wasn't there at all. *Jesus jesus oh yes please jesus*. Then something different, not a word but pure pain, clear as water, an animal's at the moment the trap closes.

It's like death, I thought, the bad part isn't the thing itself but being a witness. I suppose they could hear us too, the times before. But I never say anything.

Chapter Ten

The sunset had been red, reddish purple, and the next day
the sun held as I guessed it would; without a radio or a barometer you have to make your own prophecies. It was the second day of the week, I was ticking them off in my head,
prisoner's scratches on the wall; I felt stretched, pulled tight
like a drying rope, the fact that he had not yet appeared only
increased the possibility that he would. The seventh day
seemed a great distance away.

I wanted to get them off the island, to protect them from
him, to protect him from them, save all of them from knowledge. They might start to explore, cut other trails; already
they were beginning to be restless: fire and food, the only two
necessities, were taken care of and there was nothing left to
be done. Sun rising, drifting across the sky, shadows changing
without help, uninterrupted air, absence of defining borders,
the only break an occasional distant plane, vapour streak, for
them it must have been like living in a hammock.

In the morning David fished from the dock, catching nothing; Anna read, she was on her fourth or fifth paperback. I
swept the floor, the broom webbing itself with long threads,
dark and light, from where Anna and I brushed our hair in
front of the mirror; then I tried to work. Joe stayed on the
wall bench, arms wrapped around his knees in lawn-dwarf

position, watching me. Every time I glanced up his eyes would be there, blue as ball point pens or Superman; even with my head turned away I could feel his x-ray vision prying under my skin, a slight prickling sensation as though he was tracing me. It was hard to concentrate; I re-read two of the folk tales, about the king who learned to speak with animals and the fountain of life, but I got no further than a rough sketch of a thing that looked like a football player. It was supposed to be a giant.

"What's wrong?" I said to him finally, putting down my brush, giving up.

"Nothing," he said. He took the cover off the butter dish and started carving holes in the butter with his forefinger.

I should have realized much earlier what was happening, I should have got out of it when we were still in the city. It was unfair of me to stay with him, he'd become used to it, hooked on it, but I didn't realize that and neither did he. When you can't tell the difference between your own pleasure and your pain then you're an addict. I did that, I fed him unlimited supplies of nothing, he wasn't ready for it, it was too strong for him, he had to fill it up, like people isolated in a blank room who see patterns.

After lunch they all sat around expectantly, as though waiting for me to dole out the crayons and plasticine or regiment the sing-song, tell them what to play. I searched through the past: what did we do when it was sunny and there was no work?

"How would you like," I said, "to pick some blueberries?" Offering it as a surprise; work disguised in some other form, it had to be a game.

They seized on it, glad of the novelty. "A groove," David said. Anna and I made peanut butter sandwiches for a mid-afternoon snack; then we basted our noses and the lobes of our ears with Anna's suntan lotion and started out.

David and Anna went in the green canoe, we took the heavier one. They still couldn't paddle very well but there wasn't much wind. I had to use a lot of energy just to keep us pointed straight, because Joe didn't know how to steer; also he wouldn't admit it, which made it harder.

We wavered around the stone point where the trail goes; then we were in the archipelago of islands, tips of sunken hills, once possibly a single ridge before the lake was flooded. None of them is big enough to have a name; some are no more than rocks, with a few trees clutched and knotted to them by the roots. On one of them, further along, was the heron colony. I had to strain my eyes to spot it: the young in the nests were keeping their serpent necks and blade heads immobile, imitating dead branches. The nests were all in a single tree, white pine, grouped for mutual protection like bungalows on the outskirts. If the herons get within pecking range they fight.

"See them?" I said to Joe, pointing.

"See what?" he said. He was sweating, overworked, the wind was against us. He scowled up at the sky but he couldn't make them out until one of them lifted and settled, wings balancing.

Beyond the herons' island was a larger one, flattish, with several red pines rising straight as masts from a ground harsh with blueberry bushes. We landed and tied the canoes and I gave each of them a tin cup. The blueberries were only beginning to ripen, the dots of them showing against the green like first rain pocking the lake. I took my own cup and started to work along the shore, they ripen earlier there.

During the war or was it after they would pay us a cent a cup; there was nowhere to spend it, I didn't understand at first what the metal discs were for: leaves on one side and a man's head chopped off at the neck on the reverse.

I was remembering the others who used to come. There weren't many of them on the lake even then, the government had put them somewhere else, corralled them, but there was one family left. Every year they would appear on the lake in blueberry season and visit the good places the same way we did, condensing as though from the air, five or six of them in a weatherbeaten canoe: father in the stern, head wizened and corded like a dried root, mother with her gourd body and hair pared back to her nape, the rest children or grandchildren. They would check to see how many blueberries there were, faces neutral and distanced, but when they saw that we were picking they would move on, gliding unhurried along near the shore and then disappearing around a point or into a bay as though they had never been there. No one knew where they lived during the winter; once though we passed two of the children standing by the side of the road with tin cans of blueberries for sale. It never occurred to me till now that they must have hated us.

The shore bushes rustled: it was Joe, coming down behind me. He squatted on the stone beside me; his cup was only a third full, sprinkled with leaves and green-white berries.

"Take a rest," he said.

"In a minute." I was almost finished. It was hot, light glared from the lake; in the sun the berries were so blue they seemed lit up from within. Falling into the cup they made a plink like water.

"We should get married," Joe said.

I set the cup down carefully on the rock and turned to look at him, shielding my eyes. I wanted to laugh, it was incongruous, it wasn't what he would call his trip, the legal phrases and the paperwork and the vows, especially the finality; and he'd got the order wrong, he'd never asked whether I loved him, that was supposed to come first, I would have been prepared for that. "Why?" I said. "We're living together anyway. We don't need a certificate for that."

"I think we should," he said, "we might as well."

"But it wouldn't make any difference," I said. "Everything would be the same."

"Then why not do it?" He had moved closer, he was being logical, he was threatening me with something. I swivelled, scouting for help, but they were at the far end of the island, Anna's pink shirt tiny and blazing like a gas station banner.

"No," I said, the only answer to logic. It was because I didn't want to, that's why it would gratify him, it would be a sacrifice, of my reluctance, my distaste.

"Sometimes," he said, placing the words evenly and deliberately, pegs in a peg-board, "I get the feeling you don't give a shit about me."

"I do," I said. "I do give a shit about you," repeating it like a skipping rhyme. I wondered if that was the equivalent of saying I loved him. I was calculating how much getaway money I had in the bank, how long it would take me to pack and move out, away from the clay dust and the cellar mould smell and the monstrous humanoid pots, how soon I could find a new place. Prove your love, they say. You really want to marry me, let me fuck you instead. You really want to fuck, let me marry you instead. As long as there's a victory, some flag I can wave, parade I can have in my head.

"No, you don't, I can tell," he said, unhappy rather than angry; that was worse, I could cope with his anger. He was growing larger, becoming alien, three-dimensional; panic began.

"Look," I said, "I've been married before and it didn't work out. I had a baby too." My ace, voice patient. "I don't want to go through that again." It was true, but the words were coming out of me like the mechanical words from a talking doll, the kind with the pull tape at the back; the whole speech was unwinding, everything in order, a spool. I would always be able to say what I'd just finished saying: I've tried and failed, I'm inoculated, exempt, classified as wounded. It wasn't that I didn't suffer, I was conscientious about that, that's what qualified me. But marriage was like playing Monopoly or doing crossword puzzles, either your mind worked that way, like Anna's, or it didn't; and I'd proved mine didn't. A small neutral country.

"It would be different with us," he said, disregarding what I said about the baby.

At my wedding we filled out forms, name, age, birthplace, blood type. We had it in a post office, a J.P. did it, oil portraits of former postmasters presided from the beige walls. I could recall the exact smells, glue and humid socks and the odour of second-day blouse and crystallized deodorant from the irritated secretary, and, from another doorway, the chill of antiseptic. It was a hot day, when we stepped out into the sun we couldn't see for an instant; then there was a flock of draggled pigeons pecking at the scuffed post office lawn beside the fountain. The fountain had dolphins and a cherub with part of the face missing.

"It's over," he said, "feel better?"

He coiled his arms around me, protecting me from something, the future, and kissed me on the forehead. "You're cold," he said. My legs were shaking so much I could hardly stand up and there was an ache, slow like a groan. "Come on," he said, "we'd better get you home." He lifted my face, scrutinizing it in the light. "Maybe I should carry you to the car."

He was talking to me as though I was an invalid, not a bride. In one hand I carried a purse or a suitcase; the other was closed. We walked through the pigeons and they blew up around us, confetti. In the car I didn't cry, I didn't want to look at him. "I know it's tough," he said, "but it's better this way." Quote, unquote. His flexible hands on the wheel. It turned, perfect circle, and the gears interlocked and spun, the engine ticked like a clock, the voice of reason.

"Why are you doing this to me?" I said, losing control. "You'll ruin it." Then I was sorry, as though I'd stepped on a small animal by accident, he was so miserable: he'd abdicated, betrayed what I'd assumed were his principles, in order to be saved, by me, from me, and he'd got nothing by it.

I took his hand; he let me hold it, frowning at me, sullen as a doormat. "I'm not good enough for you," I said, motto, the words printed on a scroll like a fortune cookie. I kissed him on the side of the face. I was stalling for time, also I was afraid of him: the look he gave me as I drew away was one of baffled rage.

82

We were sitting outside in the chicken wire enclosure; Joe was in the sandbox with his back half-turned to us, scraping together a large mound of sand. He'd finished his pie, the rest of us were still eating. It was too hot to eat in the house, we had to keep the stove going for two hours. They had purple mouths and blue teeth which showed when they talked or laughed.

"That's the best pie I ever ate," David said. "Just like mother used to make." He smacked his lips and posed, pretending to be a T.V. ad.

"Stuff it," Anna said, "you can't afford just one measly compliment, can you?"

David's purple mouth grinned. "Aw," he said, "that *was* a compliment."

"The hell," Anna said. "I've met your mother."

David sighed and leaned back against his tree, rolling his eyes to Joe for sympathy. But he got none and so he gazed up at the sky instead. "This is the life," he said after a while. "We ought to start a colony, I mean a community up here, get it together with some other people, break away from the urban nuclear family. It wouldn't be a bad country if only we could kick out the fucking pig Americans, eh? Then we could have some peace."

Nobody answered him; he took off one of his shoes and began scratching the sole of his foot thoughtfully.

"I think it would be a copout," Anna said abruptly.

"What would?" David said, overly tolerant, as though she'd interrupted him in mid-sentence. "Kicking out the pigs?"

"Oh shit," Anna said, "you just won't."

"What the hell are you talking about?" he said, feigning hurt. But she sat hugging her knees, smoke breathing through her nostrils. I got up and started to collect the plates.

"It turns me on when she bends over," David said. "She's got a neat ass. I'm really into the whole ass thing. Joe, don't you think she's got a neat ass?"

"You can have it," Joe said. He was levelling the sand mound he had built, he was still angry.

I scraped the ends of crust into the stove and washed the plates, the water turning reddish blue, vein colour. The others ambled in; they didn't feel like playing bridge, they sat around the table reading detective novels and back issues of magazines, *Maclean's* and *The National Geographic*, some of them were ten years old. I'd read them all so I went into David's and Anna's room with a candle to look for more.

I had to climb up on the bed to reach the shelf. There was a high pile of books; I lifted it down to where the candle was. On top was a layer of paperbacks, the average kind, but underneath them were some things that were out of place: the brown leather photo album that ought to have been in a trunk in the city, along with my mother's unused wedding presents, tarnished silver bowls and lace tablecloths, and the scrapbooks we used to draw in when it rained. I thought she'd thrown them out; I wondered who had brought them here, which one of them.

There were several scrapbooks; I sat down on the bed and opened one at random, feeling as though I was opening someone else's private diary. It was my brother's: explosions in red and orange, soldiers dismembering in the air, planes and tanks; he must have been going to school by then, he knew enough to draw little swastikas on the sides. Further on there were flying men with comic-book capes and explorers on another planet, he spent hours explaining these pictures to me. The purple jungles I'd forgotten, the green sun with seven red moons, the animals with scales and spines and tentacles; and a man-eating plant, engulfing a careless victim, a balloon with HELP in it squeezing out of his mouth like bubble gum. The other explorers were rescuing him with their weapons: flame-throwers, trumpet-shaped pistols, ray-guns. In the background was their spaceship, bristling with gadgets.

The next scrapbook was mine. I searched through it carefully, looking for something I could recognize as myself, where

I had come from or gone wrong; but there were no drawings at all, just illustrations cut from magazines and pasted in. They were ladies, all kinds: holding up cans of cleanser, knitting, smiling, modelling toeless high heels and nylons with dark seams and pillbox hats and veils. A lady was what you dressed up as on Hallowe'en when you couldn't think of anything else and didn't want to be a ghost; or it was what you said at school when they asked you what you were going to be when you grew up, you said "A lady" or "A mother," either one was safe; and it wasn't a lie, I did want to be those things. On some of the pages were women's dresses clipped from mail order catalogues, no bodies in them.

I tried another one: mine also, earlier. The drawings were of ornately-decorated Easter eggs, singly and in groups. Some of them had people-shaped rabbits climbing up them on rope ladders; apparently the rabbits lived inside the eggs, there were doors at the tops, they could pull the ladders up after them. Beside the larger eggs were smaller ones connected to them by bridges, the outhouses. Page after page of eggs and rabbits, grass and trees, normal and green, surrounding them, flowers blooming, sun in the upper right-hand corner of each picture, moon symmetrically in the left. All the rabbits were smiling and some were laughing hilariously; several were shown eating ice-cream cones from the safety of their egg-tops. No monsters, no wars, no explosions, no heroism. I couldn't remember ever having drawn these pictures. I was disappointed in myself: I must have been a hedonistic child, I thought, and quite stodgy also, interested in nothing but social welfare. Or perhaps it was a vision of Heaven.

Behind me someone came into the room, it was David. "Hey lady," he said, "what're you doing in my bed? You a customer or something?"

"Sorry," I said. I put the album back on the shelf but I took the scrapbooks into my room and hid them under the mattress, I didn't want them spying.

Chapter Eleven

At night Joe kept turned away from me, he wasn't going to compromise. I ran my fingers over his furry back to show I wanted a truce, the borders restored to where they'd been, but after he twitched me off and grunted irritably I withdrew. I curled up, concentrating on excluding him: he was merely an object in the bed, like a sack or a large turnip. There's more than one way to skin a cat, my father used to say; it bothered me, I didn't see why they would want to skin a cat even one way. I stared at the wall and thought of maxims: two can play that game, marry in haste, repent at leisure, least said soonest mended, traditional wisdom which was never any help.

At breakfast he ignored me and the others too, hunching over his plate, mumbling replies.

"What's with him?" David said. His new beard was sprouting, a brown smudge on his chin.

"Shut up," Anna said; but she glanced at me, inquisitive, holding me responsible for it whatever it was.

Joe wiped his sweat shirt sleeve across his mouth and went out of the house, letting the screen door slam behind him.

"Maybe he's constipated," David said, "it makes them grouchy. You sure he's been getting enough exercise?" Then he went "Arf, arf" like Popeye, wiggling his ears.

"Stupid," Anna said fondly; she rumpled his hair.

"Hey, don't do that," he said, "it'll all fall out." He jumped up and went to the mirror and rearranged the hair down over his forehead; I hadn't noticed before that he combed it that way to cover the patches where it had once grown.

I gathered up the bacon rinds and the crusts from the toast and took them out to the bird tray. The jays were there, they saw I had food and told each other about it with hoarse cries. I stood quietly with my hand outstretched but they wouldn't fly down; they winged overhead, reconnoitring. Perhaps I was moving without knowing it, you had to convince them you were a thing, not an enemy. Our mother made us watch from inside the house, she said we frightened them. Once people believed the flight of birds was a portent: augury.

I heard the mosquito whine of a motor approaching; I left my handful of crumbs on the tray and went out on the point to watch. It was Paul's boat, white-painted and squarish, hand-made; he waved to me from the stern. There was another man with him, sitting in the bow, backwards.

They pulled in to the dock and I ran down the steps to greet them; I caught the rope and tied it. "Careful," I said as they stepped out, "it's rotten in places."

Paul had brought me a huge wad of vegetables from his garden: he handed me a bouquet of swiss chard, a quart basket of green beans, a bundle of carrots, a brain-sized cauliflower, bashfully, as though the gift might not be acceptable. The proper reply would have been an equally large or perhaps larger assortment. I thought with dismay of the spindly broccoli and the radishes already gone to seed.

"Here is a man," he said. "They send him to me because I know your father." He stepped backwards, effacing himself, and almost slipped off the dock.

"Malmstrom," the man said as though it was a secret code; his hand shot towards me. I transferred the swiss chard to the crook of my arm and took the hand, which squeezed mine confidentially. "Bill Malmstrom, please call me Bill." He had trimmed grey hair and an executive moustache like the shirt ads, the vodka ads; his clothes were woodsy, semi-worn, verging on the authentic. Slung around his neck was a pair of binoculars in a suede case.

We walked to the land; he had taken out a pipe and was lighting it. I wondered if he was from the government. "Paul, here, was telling me," he said, looking around for Paul, "what a nice place you have."

"It's my father's," I said.

His face drooped into the appropriate downward curve; if he'd been wearing a hat he would have taken it off. "Ah yes," he said, "a tragedy." I distrusted him: I couldn't place the accent, the name sounded German.

"Where are you from?" I asked, trying to be polite.

"Michigan," he said as though it was something to be proud of. "I'm a member of the Detroit branch of the Wildlife Protection Association of America; we have a branch in this country, quite a flourishing little branch." He beamed at me, condescending. "As a matter of fact that's what I wanted to discuss with you. Our place on Lake Erie is, ah, giving out so to say. I believe I can speak for the rest of the Michigan members in saying we'd be prepared to make you an offer."

"What for?" I said. He sounded as though he wanted me to buy something, a magazine or a membership.

He swept his pipe in a semi-circle. "This lovely piece of property," he said. "What we'd use it for would be a kind of retreat lodge, where the members could meditate and observe," he puffed, "the beauties of Nature. And maybe do a little hunting and fishing."

"Don't you want to see it?" I asked. "I mean, the house and all."

"I must admit that I've already seen it; we've had our eye on this piece for quite some time. I've been coming up here to fish for years, and I've taken the liberty, when no one seemed to be here, of having a stroll around." He gave a small harumph, a voyeur of good social standing caught in the act; then he named a price that meant I could forget about *Quebec Folk*

Tales and children's books and everything else, at least for a while.

"Would you change it?" I asked. I foresaw motels, high-rises.

"Well, we'd have to install a power generator, of course, and a septic tank; but apart from that, no, I expect we'd like to leave it the way it is, it has a definite," he stroked his moustache, "rural charm."

"I'm sorry but it's not for sale," I said, "not right now; maybe later." If my father had been dead he might have liked the proposal but as it was he would be furious if he returned and found I'd sold his house. I wasn't sure I'd be the owner in any case. There must be deeds hidden, property titles, legal papers, I'd never had any dealings with lawyers; I would have to sign forms or charters, I might have to pay death duties.

"Well," he said with the heartiness of a loser. "I'm sure the offer will still be open. Indefinitely, you might say." He drew out his wallet and gave me a card: *Bill Malmstrom, Teenie Town*, it said, *Togs for Toddlers 'n Tots.*

"Thank you," I said, "I'll keep it in mind."

I took Paul by the arm and led him to the garden, as though to reciprocate for the vegetables: I felt I had to explain, at least to him, he had gone to a lot of trouble for me.

"Your garden, she is not doing so good, ay?" he said, inspecting.

"No," I said, "we just got it weeded; but I want you to have . . :" I gazed desperately around, seized on a withered lettuce and presented it to him, roots and all, as gracefully as I could.

He held it, blinking, discouraged. "Madame will like that," he said.

"Paul," I said, lowering my voice, "the reason I can't sell is that my father's still alive."

"Yes?" he said, perking up. "He came back, he is here?"

"Not exactly," I said. "He's away right now, on a sort of trip; but perhaps he will be here soon." For all I could tell he might have been listening to us at that moment, from behind the raspberry canes or the burn heap.

"He went for the trees?" Paul said, hurt that he hadn't been consulted: he used to go too. "You saw him first, before?"

"No," I said, "he was gone when I got here; but he left me a note, more or less."

"Ah," he said, glancing nervously over my shoulder into the forest. It was clear he didn't believe me.

For lunch we had Paul's cauliflower and some tins, corn and fried ham. During the canned pears David said "Who were those two old guys?" He must have seen them from the window.

"It was a man who wanted to buy the place," I said.

"I bet he was a Yank," David said, "I can spot them in a crowded room."

"Yes," I said, "but he was from a wildlife association, that's who he was buying it for."

"Bullshit," David said, "he was a front man for the c.i.a."

I laughed. "No," I said; I showed him the *Teenie Town* card.

But David was serious. "You haven't seen them in operation the way I have," he said darkly, invoking his New York past.

"What would they want up here?" I said.

"A snooping base," he said, "bird-watchers, binoculars, it all fits. They know this is the kind of place that will be strategically important during the war."

"What war?" I asked, and Anna said "Here we go."

"It's obvious. They're running out of water, clean water, they're dirtying up all of theirs, right? Which is what we have a lot of, this country is almost all water if you look at a map. So in a while, I give it ten years, they'll be up against the wall. They'll try to swing a deal with the government, get us to give them the water cheap or for nothing in exchange for more soapflakes or something, and the government will give in, they'll be a bunch of puppets as usual. But by that time the

Twelve

l was full; I carried it to the garden to pour the
nto the trench. Joe was lying by himself on the
wn; when I came to rinse the pail he didn't move.
me on the steps, wearing her orange bikini, oiled
ritual.

bin I set the pail under the counter. David was
s chin bristles in the mirror; he slid his arm half
nd said in a guttural voice, "Come wiz me to zee

t now," I said, "I have to do some work."
d regret. "Ah well," he said, "some other time."
t my samsonite case and sat down at the table.
ver my shoulder. "Where's old Joe?"
the dock," I said.
out of sorts," David said, "maybe he has worms;
back to the city you should take him to the vet."
ent later, "How come you never laugh at my

around while I set out the brushes and paper.
id, "Well, Nature calls," and soft-shoed out the
end of a vaudeville act.
d the caps back onto the paint tubes, I had no
working: now they were all out of the way I
for the will, the deed, the property title. Paul

Nationalist Movement will be strong enough so they'll force
the government to back down; riots or kidnappings or something. Then the Yank pigs will send in the Marines, they'll
have to; people in New York and Chicago will be dropping
like flies, industry will be stalled, there'll be a black market in
water, they'll be shipping it in tankers from Alaska. They'll
come in through Quebec, it will have separated by then; the
Pepsis will even help them, they'll be having a good old laugh.
They'll hit the big cities and knock out communications and
take over, maybe shoot a few kids, and the Movement guer-
rillas will go into the bush and start blowing up the water
pipelines the Yanks will be building in places like this, to
get the water down there."

He seemed very positive about it, as if it had happened
already. I thought about the survival manuals: if the Movement guerillas were anything like David and Joe they would
never make it through the winters. They couldn't get help
from the cities, they would be too far, and the people there
would be apathetic, they wouldn't mind another change of
flag. If they tried at the outlying farms the farmers would take
after them with shotguns. The Americans wouldn't even have
to defoliate the trees, the guerillas would die of starvation and
exposure anyway.

"Where will you get food?" I said.

"What do you mean 'you'?" he said. "I'm just speculating."

I thought of how it would appear in the history books
when it was over: a paragraph with dates and a short summary
of what happened. That's how it was in high school, they
taught it neutrally, a long list of wars and treaties and alli-
ances, people taking and losing power over other people; but
nobody would ever go into the motives, why they wanted it,
whether it was good or bad. They used long words like "de-
marcation" and "sovereignty", they wouldn't say what they
meant and you couldn't ask: in high school the right thing
was to stare fixedly at the teacher as though at a movie screen,
and it was worse for a girl to ask questions than for a boy. If

a boy asked a question the other boys would make derisive sucking noises with their mouths, but if a girl asked one the other girls would say "Think you're so great" in the washroom afterwards. In the margins around the Treaty of Versailles I drew ornaments, plants with scrolled branches, hearts and stars instead of flowers. I got so I could draw invisibly, my fingers scarcely moving.

The generals and the historic moments looked better framed. If you put your eye down close to the photograph they disintegrated into grey dots.

Anna was squeezed in beside David on the bench, playing with one of his hands while he talked. "Did I ever tell you that you have Murderer's Thumb?" she said.

"Don't interrupt," he said, but when she made a whimpering face he said "Yep, you did, almost every day," and patted her arm.

"It's spread flat at the end," she said, explaining to us.

"I hope you didn't sell out," David said to me. I shook my head. "Good girl," he said, "your heart's in the right place. And the rest of her too," he said to Joe, "I like it round and firm and fully packed. Anna, you're eating too much."

I washed and Anna dried, as usual. Suddenly Anna said "David is a schmuck. He's one of the schmuckiest people I know."

I looked around at her: her voice was like fingernails, I'd never heard her talk that way about David.

"Why?" I said. "What's wrong?" He hadn't said anything at lunch that could have upset her.

"I guess you think he's hot for you." Her mouth stretched down tight with the lips inside, a toad's.

"No," I said, bewildered, "why would I think that?"

"Those things he says, you know, like about your ass and being fully packed," she said impatiently.

"I thought he was teasing." I had thought that too, it was just a habit like picking your nose, only verbal.

"Teasing, shit. He was doing it to me. He always does stuff

like that to other women i
me in the room if he could
else and tells me about it

"Oh," I said. I hadn't
does he tell you?"

Anna brooded, her di
honest. What a turd. Whe
possessive and I shouldn'
bourgeois, it's a leftover fr
should all be swingers and
these basic emotions, if yo
out, right?" It was an arti
lenging me to affirm or de
anything. "He pretends he
cool," she said, "but really
and get away with it, I ca
about it is coverup bullsh
smiling, friendly again. "I t
know if he grabs you or a
with you, it's all about me

"Thank you," I said. I wa
to believe that what they ca
possible, for someone. But
knew in her place I would
her take care of herself, My
me of zoos and insane asylu

Chapter

The slop p
dirty water
dock, face
Anna passe
for her su

In the
pondering
around me
outhouse."

"Not ri
He mi
I took
He leaned
"Down
"He see
when you
And a m
jokes?"

He hu
Finally he
door like

I swive
intention
would sea

had been certain he was dead, that made me doubt my theory. Perhaps the c.i.a. had done away with him to get the land, Mr. Malmstrom was not quite plausible; but that was preposterous, I couldn't start suspecting people for no reason.

I rummaged in the cavity under the wall bench, went through the shelves, groped under the beds where the tents were stored. He might have filed the papers in a safety-deposit box, earlier, in a city bank, I'd never find them. Or he might have burned them. At any rate they weren't here.

Unless they were in among the pages of a book: I checked Goldsmith and Burns, holding them by the spines and shaking, then I thought of his lunatic drawings, the only clue I had that he might not be dead. I'd never gone through all of them. In a way that would be the logical hiding place; he'd always been logical, and madness is only an amplification of what you already are.

I lifted down the stack of drawings and began to look. The paper was thin and soft, like rice paper. First the hands and antlered figures, always with numbers scrawled in the corner, then a larger sheet, a half-moon with four sticks coming out of it, bulbed at the ends. I righted the page, judging by the numbers, and it became a boat with people, the knobs were their heads. It was reassuring to find I could interpret it, it made sense.

But the next one was nothing I could recognize. The body was long, a snake or a fish; it had four limbs or arms and a tail and on the head were two branched horns. Lengthwise it was like an animal, an alligator; upright it was more human, but only in the positions of the arms and the front-facing eyes.

Total derangement. I wondered when it had started; it must have been the snow and the loneliness, he'd pushed himself too far, it gets in through your eyes, the thin black cold of mid-winter night, the white days dense with sunlight, outer space melting and freezing again into different shapes, your mind starts doing the same thing. The drawing was something he saw, a hallucination; or it might have been himself, what he thought he was turning into.

I uncovered the next page. But it wasn't a drawing, it was a typed letter, I skimmed it quickly. Addressed to my father.

Dear Sir:

Many thanks for forwarding the photographs and tracings and the corresponding map. The material is most valuable and I shall include some of it in my forthcoming work on the subject, with your permission and giving due credit. Details of any subsequent discoveries you may make would be most welcome.

I include a copy of one of my recent studies which you may find of interest.

Yours sincerely.

The letter had an illegible signature and a university crest. Paperclipped to it were half a dozen xeroxed sheets: *Rock Paintings of the Central Shield, by Dr. Robin M. Grove.* The first few pages were maps and graphs and statistics; I skimmed them quickly. At the end of the article there were three short paragraphs, subtitled *Aesthetic Qualities and Possible Significance.*

The subject matter falls into the following categories: Hands, Abstract Symbols, Humans, Animals and Mythological Creatures. In treatment they are reminiscent, with their elongated limbs and extreme distortion, of the drawings of children. The static rigidity is in marked contrast to the rock paintings of other cultures, most notably the European cave paintings.

From the above features we may deduce that the creators of the paintings were interested exclusively in symbolic content, at the expense of expressiveness and form. However we can only indulge in conjecture as to the nature of this content, since no historical records exist. Informants questioned have supplied conflicting traditions. Some state that the sites of the paintings are the abodes of powerful or protective spirits, which may ex-

*plain the custom, persisting in remote areas, of leaving
offerings of clothing and small bundles of "prayer" sticks.
One gives more credence to the theory that the paintings
are associated with the practice of fasting to produce significant or predictive dreams.*

*Doubtful also is the technique employed. The paint-
ings seem to have been executed either with the fingers or
with a crude brush of some sort. The predominant colour
is red, with minor occurrences of white and yellow; this
may be due either to the fact that red among the Indians
is a sacred colour or to the relative availability of iron
oxides. The bonding agent is being investigated; it may
prove to be bears' fat or birds' eggs, or perhaps blood or
spittle.*

The academic prose breathed reason; my hypotheses
crumbled like sand. This was the solution, the explanation:
he never failed to explain.

His drawings were not originals then, only copies. He must
have been doing them as a sort of retirement hobby, he was an
incurable amateur and enthusiast: if he'd become hooked on
these rock paintings he would have combed the area for them,
collecting them with his camera, pestering the experts by
letter whenever he found one; an old man's delusion of use-
fulness.

I pressed my fingers into my eyes, hard, to make the pool
of blackness ringed with violent colour. Release, red spreading back in, abrupt as pain. The secret had come clear, it had
never been a secret, I'd made it one, that was easier. My eyes
came open, I began to arrange.

I thought, I suppose I knew it from the beginning, I
shouldn't have tried to find out, it's killed him. I had the
proof now, indisputable, of sanity and therefore of death.
Relief, grief, I must have felt one or the other. A blank, a
disappointment: crazy people can come back, from wherever
they go to take refuge, but dead people can't, they are prohibited. I tried to recall him, picture his face, the way he'd

been when he was alive, I found I couldn't; all I could see was
the cards he used to hold up, testing us: $3 \times 9 =$? He was as
absent now as a number, a zero, the question mark in place of
the missing answer. Unknown quantity. His way. Everything
had to be measured.

I was staring down at the drawings, they were framed by
my two arms lain parallel on the table. I began to notice them
again. There was a gap, something not accounted for, something left over.

I spread the first six pages out on the table and studied
them, using what they called my intelligence, it shortcircuits
those other things. The notes and numbers were apparently
a location code, it was like a puzzle he'd left for me to solve,
an arithmetic problem; he taught us arithmetic, our mother
taught us to read and write. Geometry, the first thing I learned
was how to draw flowers with compasses, they were like acid
patterns. Once they thought you could see God that way but
all I saw was landscapes and geometrical shapes; which would
be the same thing if you believed God was a mountain or a
circle. He said Jesus was a historical figure and God was a
superstition, and a superstition was a thing that didn't exist.
If you tell your children God doesn't exist they will be forced
to believe you are the god, but what happens when they find
out you are human after all, you have to grow old and die?
Resurrection is like plants, Jesus Christ is risen today they
sang at Sunday School, celebrating the daffodils; but people
are not onions, as he so reasonably pointed out, they stay
under.

The numbers were a system, a game; I would play it with
him, it would make him seem less dead. I lined up the pages
and compared the notes, carefully as a jeweller.

On one of the drawings, another antlered figure, I finally
spotted the key: a name I recognized, White Birch Lake where
we went bass fishing, it was connected to the main lake by a
portage. I went into David's and Anna's room where the map
of the district was tacked to the wall. Marked on a point of
land was a tiny red x and a number, identical with the number

on the drawing. The printed name was different, *Lac des Verges Blanches*, the government had been translating all the English names into French ones, though the Indian names remained the same. Scattered here and there were other xs, like a treasure map.

I wanted to go there and verify, match the drawing with reality; that way I'd be sure I'd followed the rules and done it right. I could disguise it as a fishing trip, David hadn't caught anything since his first attempt, though he'd been trying. We'd have time to go there and get back with two days to spare.

I heard Anna's voice approaching, singing, the words trailing off as her breath gave out climbing the steps. I went back to the main room.

"Hi," she said, "do I look burnt?"

She was pink now, parboiled, white showing around the orange edges of her suit, neck dividing body colour from applied face colour. "A little," I said.

"Listen," she said, her voice shifting into concern, "what's wrong with Joe? I was down on the dock with him and he didn't say one word."

"He doesn't talk much," I said.

"I know, but this was different. He was just lying there." She was pushing, demanding answers.

"He thinks we should get married," I said.

Her eyebrows lifted like antennae. "Really? Joe? That's not. . . ."

"I don't want to."

"Oh," she said, "then that's awful. You must feel awful." She'd found out; now she was rubbing after-sun lotion on her shoulders. "Mind?" she said, handing me the plastic tube.

I didn't feel awful; I realized I didn't feel much of anything, I hadn't for a long time. Perhaps I'd been like that all my life, just as some babies are born deaf or without a sense of touch; but if that was true I wouldn't have noticed the absence. At some point my neck must have closed over, pond freezing or a wound, shutting me into my head; since then everything had been glancing off me, it was like being in a vase, or the village where I could see them but not hear them because I couldn't understand what was being said. Bottles distort for the observer too: frogs in the jam jar stretched wide, to them watching I must have appeared grotesque.

"Thanks," Anna said, "I hope I won't peel. I think you should go talk to him, or something."

"I have," I said; but her eyes were accusing, I hadn't done enough, conciliation, expiation. I went obediently towards the door.

"Maybe you can work it out," she called after me.

Joe was still on the dock but he was sitting on the edge now with his feet in the water, I crouched down beside him. His toes had dark hairs on the tops, spaced like the needles on a balsam twig.

"What is it?" I said. "Are you sick?"

"You know fucking well," he said after a minute.

"Let's go back to the city," I said, "the way it was before." I took hold of his hand so I could feel the calloused palm, thickened by the wheel, concrete.

"You're screwing around with me," he said, still not looking at me. "All I want is a straight answer."

"About what?" I said. Near the dock there were some water skippers, surface tension holding them up; the fragile shadows of the dents where their feet touched fell on the sand underwater, moving when they moved. His vulnerability embarrassed me, he could still feel, I should have been more careful with him.

"Do you love me, that's all," he said. "That's the only thing that matters."

It was the language again, I couldn't use it because it wasn't mine. He must have known what he meant but it was an imprecise word; the Eskimoes had fifty-two names for snow because it was important to them, there ought to be as many for love.

"I want to," I said. "I do in a way." I hunted through my brain for any emotion that would coincide with what I'd said. I did want to, but it was like thinking God should exist and not being able to believe.

"Fucking jesus," he said, pulling his hand away, "just yes or no, don't mess around."

"I'm trying to tell the truth," I said. The voice wasn't mine, it came from someone dressed as me, imitating me.

"The truth is," he said bitterly, "you think my work is crap, you think I'm a loser and I'm not worth it." His face contorted, it was pain: I envied him.

"No," I said, but I couldn't say it right and he needed more than that.

"Come up to the cabin," I said; Anna was there, she would help. "I'll make some tea." I got up but he wouldn't follow.

While the stove was heating I took the leather album from the shelf in their room and opened it on the table, where Anna was reading. It was no longer his death but my own that concerned me; perhaps I would be able to tell when the change occurred by the differences in my former faces, alive up to a year, a day, then frozen. The duchess at the French court before the Revolution, who stopped laughing or crying so her skin would never change or wrinkle, it worked, she died immortal.

Grandmothers and grandfathers first, distant ancestors, strangers, in face-front firing-squad poses: cameras weren't ordinary then, maybe they thought their souls were being stolen, as the Indians did. Underneath them were labels in white, my mother's cautious printing. My mother before she was married, another stranger, with bobbed hair and a knitted hat. Wedding pictures, corseted smiles. My brother before I was born, then pictures of me beginning to appear. Paul taking us down the lake with his sleigh and horses before the ice went out. My mother, in her leather jacket and odd long 1940s hair, standing beside the tray for the birds, her hand stretched out; the jays were there too, she's training them, one is on her shoulder, peering at her with clever thumbtack eyes, another is landing on her wrist, wings caught as a blur. Sun sifting around her through the pines, her eyes looking straight at the camera, frightened, receding into the shadows of her head like a skull's, a trick of the light.

I watched myself grow larger. Mother and father in alternate shots, building the house, walls and then the roof, planting the garden. Around them were borders of blank paper, at each corner a hinge, they were like small grey and white windows opening into a place I could no longer reach. I was in most of the pictures, shut in behind the paper; or not me but the missing part of me.

School pictures, my face lined up with forty others, colossal teachers towering above us. I could find myself always, I was the one smudged with movement or turning the other way. Further on, glossy colour prints, forgotten boys with pimples and carnations, myself in the stiff dresses, crinolines and tulle, layered like store birthday cakes; I was civilized at last, the finished product. She would say "You look very nice, dear," as though she believed it; but I wasn't convinced, I knew by then she was no judge of the normal.

"Is that you?" Anna said, putting down *The Mystery At Sturbridge*. "Christ, how could we ever wear that stuff?"

The last pages of the album were blank, with some loose prints stuck in between the black leaves as though my mother hadn't wanted to finish. After the formal dresses I disappeared; no wedding pictures, but of course we hadn't taken any. I closed the cover, straightening the edges.

No hints or facts, I didn't know when it had happened. I must have been all right then; but after that I'd allowed myself to be cut in two. Woman sawn apart in a wooden crate, wearing a bathing suit, smiling, a trick done with mirrors, I read it in a comic book; only with me there had been an accident and I came apart. The other half, the one locked away, was the only one that could live; I was the wrong half, detached, terminal. I was nothing but a head, or no, something minor like a severed thumb; numb. At school they used to play a joke, they would bring little boxes with cotton wool in them and a hole cut in the bottom; they would poke their finger through the hole and pretend it was a dead finger.

Chapter Thirteen

We pushed off from the dock at ten by David's watch. The sky was watercolour blue, the cloud bunches white on the backs and grey on the bellies. Wind from the stern, waves over-taking, my arms lifting and swinging, light and automatic as though they knew what to do. I was at the front, figurehead; behind me Joe shoved at the water, the canoe surged forward.

The landmarks passed, unscrolling, one-dimensional map thickening into stone and wood around us: point, cliff, leaning dead tree, heron island with the intricate bird silhouettes, blueberry island sailed by its mast pines, foregrounds. On the next island there was once a trapper's cabin, logs chinked with grass and a straw mound where the bed had been; I could see nothing left but a muddle of rotting timber.

In the morning we talked, uselessly but in calm rational voices as though discussing the phone bill; which meant it was final. We were still in bed, his feet stuck out at the bottom. I could hardly wait till I was old so I wouldn't have to do this any more.

"When we get back to the city," I said, "I'll move out."

"I will if you like," he said generously.

"No, you've got all your pots and things there."

"Have it your way," he said, "you always do."

He thought of it as a contest, like the children at school who would twist your arm and say Give in? Give in? until you did; then they would let go. He didn't love me, it was an idea of himself he loved and he wanted someone to join him, anyone would do, I didn't matter so I didn't have to care.

The sun was at twelve. We had lunch on a jagged island almost out in the wide part of the lake. After we landed we found that someone had built a fireplace already, on the shore ledge of bare granite; trash was strewn around it, orange peelings and tin cans and a rancid bulge of greasy paper, the tracks of humans. It was like dogs pissing on a fence, as if the endlessness, anonymous water and unclaimed land, compelled them to leave their signature, stake their territory, and garbage was the only thing they had to do it with. I picked up the pieces of clutter and piled them to one side, I would burn them afterwards.

"That's disgusting," Anna said. "How can you touch it?"

"It's the sign of a free country," David said. "Germany under Hitler was very tidy."

We didn't need to use the axe, the island was covered with dry sticks, branches discarded from trees. I boiled the water and made tea and we had chicken noodle soup, out of a package, and sardines and tinned applesauce.

We sat in the shade, white smoke and the smell of scorching orange peels wrapping over us when the wind swerved. I hooked the billy tin off the fire and poured the tea; ashes and bits of twig were floating in it.

"Gentlemen," David said, raising his tin cup, "Up the Queen. Did that once in a bar in New York and these three Limeys came over and wanted to start a fight, they thought we were Yanks insulting their Queen. But I said she was our Queen too so we had the right, and they ended up buying us a drink."

"I think it would be more fair," Anna said, "if you did it, 'Ladies and Gentlemen, Up the Queen and the Duke.' "

"None of that Women's Lib," David said, his eyes lidding, "or you'll be out on the street. I won't have one in the house, they're preaching random castration, they get off on that, they're roving the streets in savage bands armed with garden shears."

"I'll join if you will," Anna said to me, joking.

I said "I think men ought to be superior." But neither of them heard the actual words; Anna looked at me as though I'd betrayed her and said "Wow, are you ever brainwashed," and David said "Want a job?" and to Joe, "Hear that, you're superior." But when Joe only grunted he said "You should wire him for sound. Or fix him up with a plug and a shade, he'd make a great end-table lamp. I'm having him give a guest lecture in Adult Vegetation next year, 'How Pots Communicate', he'll walk in and say nothing for two hours, that'll freak them." Joe smiled at last, wanly.

In the night I had wanted rescue, if my body could be made to sense, respond, move strongly enough, some of the red lightbulb synapses, blue neurons, incandescent molecules might seep into my head through the closed throat, neck membrane. Pleasure and pain are side by side they said but most of the brain is neutral; nerveless, like fat. I rehearsed emotions, naming them: joy, peace, guilt, release, love and hate, react, relate; what to feel was like what to wear, you watched the others and memorized it. But the only thing there was the fear that I wasn't alive: a negative, the difference between the shadow of a pin and what it's like when you stick it in your arm, in school caged in the desk I used to do that, with pen-nibs and compass points too, instruments of knowledge, English and Geometry; they've discovered rats prefer any sensation to none. The insides of my arms were stippled with tiny wounds, like an addict's. They slipped the needle into the vein and I was falling down, it was like diving, sinking from one layer of darkness to a deeper, deepest; when I rose up through the anaesthetic, pale green and then daylight, I could remember nothing.

"Don't bother him," Anna said.

"Or maybe I'll make it a short course this time," David said. "For the businessmen how to open the Playboy centrefold with the left hand only, keeping the right free for action, for the housewives how to switch on the T.V. and switch off their heads, that's all they need to know, then we can go home."

But he wouldn't, he needed to be rescued himself and neither of us would put on the cape and boots and the thunderbolt sweatshirt, we were both afraid of failure; we lay with our backs to each other, pretending to sleep, while Anna prayed to nobody through the plywood wall. Romance comic books, on the cover always a pink face oozing tears like a melting popsicle; men's magazines were about pleasure, cars and women, the skins bald as inner tubes. In a way it was a relief, to be exempt from feeling.

"The trouble with you is you hate women," Anna said savagely; she threw the rest of her tea and the tealeaves out of her tin cup into the lake, they hit with a splat.

David grinned. "That's what they call a delayed reaction," he said. "Goose Anna in the bum and three days later she squeals. Cheer up, you're so cute when you're mad." He crawled over to her on all fours and rubbed his bristly burdock chin against her face and asked her how she would like to be raped by a porcupine. "You know that one?" he said. "How do porcupines do it? Carefully!" Anna smiled at him as though he was a brain-damaged child.

The next minute he had scrambled up and was capering on the point, shaking his clenched fist and yelling "Pigs! Pigs!" as loud as he could. It was some Americans, going past on their way to the village, their boat sloshing up and down in the waves, spray pluming, flags cocked fore and aft. They couldn't hear him because of the wind and the motor, they thought he was greeting, they waved and smiled.

I washed the dishes and soaked the fireplace, the hot stones sizzling, and we packed and started again. It was rougher, there were whitecaps on the open lake, the canoe rolled under us, we had to fight to keep it from turning broadside on; foam trailed on the dark water, spent waves. Paddle digging the lake, ears filled with moving air; breath and sweat, muscle hurt, my body at any rate was alive.

The wind was too strong, we had to change course; we headed across to the lee shore and followed it, as close to the land as possible, threading the maze of rocks and shallows. It was the long way around but the trees sheltered us.

Finally we reached the narrow bay where the portage was; the sun was at four, we'd been delayed by the wind. I hoped I would be able to find the place, the beginning of the path; I knew it was on the opposite side. As we rounded the point I heard a sound, human sound. At first it was like an outboard starting; then it was a snarl. Chainsaw, I could see them now, two men in yellow helmets. They'd left a trail, trees felled at intervals into the bay, trunks cut cleanly as though by a knife.

Surveyors, the paper company or the government, the power company. If it was the power company I knew what it meant: they were going to raise the lake level as they had sixty years ago, they were plotting the new shoreline. Twenty feet up again and this time they wouldn't cut off the trees as they had before, it would cost too much, they would be left to rot. The garden would go but the cabin would survive; the hill would become an eroding sand island surrounded by dead trees.

As we went by they glanced up at us, then turned back to their work, indifferent. Advance men, agents. Swish and crackle as the tree tottered, whump and splash as it hit. Near them was a post driven into the ground, numbers on it in fresh red paint. The lake didn't matter to them, only the system: it would be a reservoir. During the war. I would be able to do nothing, I didn't live there.

The landing place at the portage was clogged with driftwood, sodden and moss-grown. We pushed in among the slippery logs as far as we could, then clambered out and waded, dragging the canoes up over, soaking our shoes. It was bad for the canoes, it scraped the keels. There were other paint marks, recent.

We unloaded the canoes and I knotted the paddles into position across the thwarts. They said they would take the tents and the canoes and Anna and I could take the packs and the leftovers, the fishing rods and the tackle box with the jar of frogs I'd caught that morning, the movie equipment. David had insisted on it, though I warned him we might tip.

"We have to use up the film," he said, "we've only got it rented for another week."

Anna said "But there won't be anything you want," and David said "How do you know what I want?"

"There's an Indian rock painting," I said, "prehistoric. You might take that." A point of interest, it would go with the Bottle Villa and the stuffed moose family, a new anomaly for their collection.

"Wow," David said, "Is there? Neat," and Anna said "For god's sake don't encourage him."

Neither of them had portaged before; we had to help them lift and balance the canoes. I said maybe they should double up, both of them under one canoe, but David insisted they could do it the real way. I said they should be careful; if the canoe slipped sideways and you didn't get out in time it would break your neck. "What's the matter," he said, "don't you trust us?"

The trail hadn't been brushed out recently but there were deep footprints, bootprints, in the muddy places. Two sets, they pointed in but not out: whoever they were, Americans maybe, spies, they were still in there.

The packs were heavy, food for three days in case the weather turned bad and marooned us; the straps cut into my shoulders, I leaned forward against the weight, feet squishing in the wet shoes as I walked.

The portage was up over a steep ridge of rock, watershed, then down through ferns and saplings to an oblong pond, a shallow mudhole we'd have to paddle across to reach the second portage. Anna and I got there first and set down the packs; Anna had time to smoke half a cigarette before David and Joe came staggering down the trail, bumping into the sides like blinkered horses. We held the canoes and they crouched out from under, they were pink and breathless.

"Better be fish in there," David said, sleeving off his forehead.

"The next one's shorter," I told them.

The water was covered with lily pads, the globular yellow lilies with their thick centre snouts pushing up from among them. It swarmed with leeches, I could see them undulating sluggishly under the brown surface. When the paddles hit bottom on the way across, gas bubbles from decomposing vegetation rose and burst with a stench of rotten eggs or farts. The air fogged with mosquitoes.

We reached the second portage, marked by a trapper's blaze weathered to the colour of the tree. I got out and stood holding the canoe steady while Joe climbed forward.

It was behind me, I smelled it before I saw it; then I heard the flies. The smell was like decaying fish. I turned around and it was hanging upside down by a thin blue nylon rope tied round its feet and looped over a tree branch, its wings fallen open. It looked at me with its mashed eye.

Chapter Fourteen

"Heavy," David said. "What is it?"

"A dead bird," Anna said. She held her nose with two fingers.

I said "It's a heron. You can't eat them." I couldn't tell how it had been done, bullet, smashed with a stone, hit with a stick. This would be a good place for herons, they would come to fish in the shallow water, standing on one leg and striking with the long spear bill. They must have got it before it had time to rise.

"We need that," David said, "we can put it next to the fish guts."

"Shit," Joe said, "it really stinks."

"That won't show in the movie," David said, "you can stand it for five minutes, it looks so great, you have to admit." They began to set up the camera; Anna and I waited, sitting on the packs.

I saw a beetle on it, blueblack and oval; when the camera whirred it burrowed in under the feathers. Carrion beetle, death beetle. Why had they strung it up like a lynch victim, why didn't they just throw it away like the trash? To prove they could do it, they had the power to kill. Otherwise it was valueless: beautiful from a distance but it couldn't be tamed or cooked or trained to talk, the only relation they could have to a thing like that was to destroy it. Food, slave or corpse, limited choices; horned and fanged heads sawed off and mounted on the billiard room wall, stuffed fish, trophies. It must have been the Americans; they were in there now, we would meet them.

The second portage was shorter but more thickly overgrown: leaves brushed, branches pushed into the corridor of air over the trail as though preventing. Newly broken stubs, wood and pith exposed like splintered bones, ferns trampled, they'd been here, their tractor-tread footsteps dinting the mud path in front of me like excavations, craters. The slope descended, slits of the lake gleamed through the trees. I wondered what I would say to them, what could be said, if I asked them why it would mean nothing. But when we reached the end of the portage they were nowhere in sight.

The lake was a narrow crescent, the far end was hidden. Lac des verges blanches, the white birch grew in clumps by the shore edge, doomed eventually by the disease, tree cancer, but not yet. The wind swayed the tops of them; it was blowing crossways over the lake. The surface corrugated, water flapping against the shore.

We got into the canoes again and paddled towards the bend; I remembered there was an open space where we could camp. On the way there were several abandoned beaver lodges shaped like dilapidated beehives or wooden haystacks; I memorized them, the bass liked underwater tangle.

We were later than I had planned, the sun was red and weakening. David wanted to fish right away but I said we had to pitch the tents and collect wood first. There was garbage at this site too but it was ancient garbage, the labels on the beer bottles illegible, the cans corroded. I gathered it up and took it with me when I went back among the trees to dig the toilet hole.

Layer of leaves and needles, layer of roots, damp sand. That was what used to bother me most about the cities, the white zero-mouthed toilets in their clean tiled cubicles. Flush toilets and vacuum cleaners, they roared and made things vanish, at that time I was afraid there was a machine that could make people vanish like that too, go nowhere, like a camera that could steal not only your soul but your body also. Levers and buttons, triggers, the machines sent them up as roots sent up flowers; tiny circles and oblongs, logic become visible, you couldn't tell in advance what would happen if you pressed them.

I showed the three of them where I had dug the hole. "Where do you sit?" Anna asked, squeamish.

"On the ground," David said, "good for you, toughen you up. You could use an ass job." Anna poked him on the belt buckle and said "Flab," imitating him.

I opened more tins and heated them, baked beans and peas, and we ate them with smokey tea. From the rock where I washed the dishes I could see part of a tent, in among the cedars at the distant end of the lake: their bunker. Binoculars trained on me, I could feel the eye rays, cross of the rifle sight on my forehead, in case I made a false move.

David was impatient, he wanted his money's worth, what he'd come for. Anna said she'd stay at the campsite: fishing didn't interest her. We left her the insect spray and the three of us got into the green canoe with the fishing rods. I put the frog jar in the stern where I could reach it. David was facing me this time; Joe sat in the bow, he was going to fish too, though he didn't have a licence.

The wind had dwindled, the lake was pink and orange. We went along the shore, birches cool, overhanging us, ice pillars. I was dizzy, too much water and sun glare, the skin of my face was shimmering as though burned, afterglow. In my head when I closed my eyes the shape of the heron dangled, upside down. I should have buried it.

The canoe steered over to the nearest beaver lodge and they tied up to it. I opened the tackle box and clipped a lure onto David's line. He was happy, whistling under his breath.

"Hey, maybe I'll hook a beaver," he said. "The national emblem. That's what they should've put on the flag instead of a maple leaf, a split beaver; I'd salute that."

"Why should it be split?" I said. It was like skinning the cat, I didn't get it.

He looked exasperated. "It's a joke," he said; and when I still didn't laugh, "Where've you been living? It's slang for cunt. The Maple Beaver for Ever, that would be neat." He lowered his line into the water and began to sing, off-key:

> In days of yore, from Britains shore
> Wolfe, the gallant hero, came:
> It spread all o'er the hooerhouse floor
> On Canada's fair domain. . . .

They sing that at your school?"

"The fish will hear you," I said, and he stopped.

A part of the body, a dead animal. I wondered what part of them the heron was, that they needed so much to kill it.

Into my head the tugboat floated, the one that was on the lake before, logboom trailing it, men waving from the cabin, sunlight and blue sky, the perfect way. But it didn't last. One spring when we got to the village it was beached near the government dock, abandoned. I wanted to see what the little house was like, how they had lived; I was sure there would be a miniature table and chairs, beds that folded down out of the walls, flowered window curtains. We climbed up; the door was open but inside it was bare wood, not even painted; there was no furniture at all and the stove was gone. The only things we could find were two rusted razor blades on the windowsill and some pictures drawn on the walls in pencil.

I thought they were plants or fish, some of them were shaped like clams, but my brother laughed, which meant he knew something I didn't; I nagged at him until he explained. I was shocked, not by those parts of the body, we'd been told about those, but that they should be cut off like that from the bodies that ought to have gone with them, as though they could detach themselves and crawl around on their own like snails.

I'd forgotten about that; but of course they were magic drawings like the ones in caves. You draw on the wall what's important to you, what you're hunting. They had enough food, no need to draw tinned peas and Argentine corned beef, and that's what they wanted instead during those monotonous and not at all idyllic trips up and down the lake, nothing to do but play cards, they must have detested it, back and forth chained to the logs. All of them dead now or old, they probably hated each other.

The bass struck on both lines at once. They fought hard, the rods doubled over. David landed one but Joe let his escape into the labyrinth of sticks, where it wound the line around a branch and snapped it.

"Hey," David was saying, "kill it for me." The bass was fierce, it was flipping around the inside of the canoe. It spat water from its undershot jaw with a hissing sound; it was either terrified or enraged, I couldn't tell which.

"You do it," I said, handing him the knife. "I showed you how, remember?"

Thud of metal on fishbone, skull, neckless headbody, the fish is whole, I couldn't any more, I had no right to. We didn't need it, our proper food was tin cans. We were committing this act, violation, for sport or amusement or pleasure, recreation they call it, these were no longer the right reasons. That's an explanation but no excuse my father used to say, a favourite maxim.

While they admired David's murder, cadaver, I took the bottle with the frogs in it out of the tackle box and unscrewed the top; they slipped into the water, green with black leopard spots and gold eyes, rescued. Highschool, each desk with a tray on it and a frog, exhaling ether, spread and pinned flat as a doily and slit open, the organs explored and clipped out, the detached heart still gulping slowly like an adam's apple, no martyr's letters on it, the intestines messy string. Pickled cat pumped full of plastic, red for the arteries, blue for the veins, at the hospital, the undertaker's. Find the brain of the worm, donate your body to science. Anything we could do to the animals we could do to each other: we practised on them first.

Joe flipped his broken line back to me and I rummaged among the lures and found another leader, a lead sinker, another hook: accessory, accomplice.

The Americans had rounded the point, two of them in a silver canoe; they were barging towards us. I assessed them, their disguises: they weren't the bloated middle-aged kind, those would stick to powerboats and guides; they were younger, trimmer, with the candid, tanned astronaut finish valued by the magazines. When they were even with us their mouths curved open, showing duplicate sets of teeth, white and even as false ones.

"Gettin' any?" the front man said with a midwestern accent; traditional greeting.

"Lots," David said, smiling back. I was expecting him to say something to them, insult them, but he didn't. They were quite large.

"Us too," the front one said. "We been in here three-four days, they been biting the whole time, caught our limit every day." They had a starry flag like all of them, a miniature decal sticker on the canoe bow. To show us we were in occupied territory.

"Well, see ya," the back one said. Their canoe moved past us towards the next beaver house.

Raygun fishing rods, faces impermeable as space-suit helmets, sniper eyes, they did it; guilt glittered on them like tinfoil. My brain recited the stories I'd been told about them: the ones who stuffed the pontoons of their seaplane with illegal fish, the ones who had a false bottom to their car, two hundred lake trout on dry ice, the game warden caught them by accident. "This is a lousy country," they said when he wouldn't take the bribe, "we ain't never coming back here." They got drunk and chased loons in their powerboats for fun, backtracking on the loon as it dived, not giving it a chance to fly, until it drowned or got chopped up in the propeller blades. Senseless killing, it was a game; after the war they'd been bored.

The sunset was fading, at the other side of the sky the black was coming up. We took the fish back, four of them by now, and I cut a Y-shaped sapling stringer to go through the gills.

"Poo," Anna said to us, "you smell like a fish market."

David said "Wish we had some beer. Maybe we could get some off the Yanks, they're the type."

I went down to the lake with the bar of soap to wash the fish blood off my hands. Anna followed me.

"God," she said, "what'm I going to do? I forgot my make-up, he'll kill me."

I studied her: in the twilight her face was grey. "Maybe he won't notice," I said.

"He'll notice, don't you worry. Not now maybe, it hasn't all rubbed off, but in the morning. He wants me to look like a young chick all the time, if I don't he gets mad."

"You could let your face get really dirty," I said.

She didn't answer that. She sat down on the rock and rested her forehead on her knees. "He'll get me for it," she said fatalistically. "He's got this little set of rules. If I break one of them I get punished, except he keeps changing them so I'm never sure. He's crazy, there's something missing in him, you know what I mean? He likes to make me cry because he can't do it himself."

"But that can't be serious," I said, "the makeup thing."

A sound came out of her throat, a cough or a laugh. "It's not just that; it's something for him to use. He watches me all the time, he waits for excuses. Then either he won't screw at all or he slams it in so hard it hurts. I guess it's awful of me to say that." Her eggwhite eyes turned towards me in the half-darkness. "But if you said any of this to him he'd just make funny cracks about it, he says I have a mind like a soap opera, he says I invent it. But I really don't, you know." She was

116

appealing to me for judgment but she didn't trust me, she was afraid I would talk to him about it behind her back.

"Maybe you should leave," I said, offering my solution, "or get a divorce."

"Sometimes I think he wants me to, I can't tell any more. It used to be good, then I started to really love him and he can't stand that, he can't stand having me love him. Isn't that funny?" She had my mother's leather jacket over her shoulders, she'd brought it because she didn't have a heavy sweater. With Anna's head attached to it it was incongruous, diminished. I tried to think about my mother but she was blanked out; the only thing that remained was a story she once told about how, when she was little, she and her sister had made wings for themselves out of an old umbrella; they'd jumped off the barn roof, attempting to fly, and she broke both her ankles. She would laugh about it but the story seemed to me then chilly and sad, the failure unbearable.

"Sometimes I think he'd like me to die," Anna said, "I have dreams about it."

We walked back and I built up the fire and mixed some cocoa, using powdered milk. Everything was dark now except for the flames, sparks going up in spirals, coals underneath pulsing red when the night breeze hit them. We sat on the groundsheets, David with his arm around Anna, Joe and I a foot apart.

"This reminds me of Girl Guides," Anna said in the cheerful voice I once thought was hers. She began to sing, the notes hesitant, quavering:

> There'll be bluebirds over
> The white cliffs of Dover
> Tomorrow, when the world is free. . . .

The words went out towards the shadows, smoke-thin, evaporating. Across the lake a barred owl was calling, quick and soft like a wing beating against the eardrum, cutting across the pattern of her voice, negating her. She glanced behind her: she felt it.

"Now everybody sing," she said, clapping her hands.

David said "Well, goodnight children," and he and Anna went into their tent. The tent lit up from inside for a moment, flashlight, then went out.

"Coming?" Joe said.

"In a minute." I wanted to give him time to go to sleep.

I sat in the dark, the stroking sound of the night lake surrounding me. In the distance the Americans' campfire glowed, a dull red cyclops eye: the enemy lines. I wished evil towards them: Let them suffer, I prayed, tip their canoe, burn them, rip them open. Owl: answer, no answer.

I crawled into the tent through the mosquito-netting; I groped for the flashlight but didn't switch it on, I didn't want to disturb him. I undressed by touch; he was obscure beside me, inert, comforting as a log. Perhaps that was the only time there could be anything like love, when he was asleep, demanding nothing. I passed my hand lightly over his shoulder as I would touch a tree or a stone.

But he wasn't sleeping; he moved, reached over for me.

"I'm sorry," I said, "I thought you were asleep."

"Okay," he said, "I give up, you win. We'll forget everything I said and do it like you want, back to the way it was before, right?"

It was too late, I couldn't. "No," I said. I had already moved out.

His hand tightened in anger on my arm; then he let go. "Sweet flaming balls of Christ," he said. His outline lifted in the darkness, I crouched down, he was going to hit me; but he turned over away from me, muffling himself in the sleeping bag.

My heart bumped, I held still, translating the noises on the other side of the canvas wall. Squeaks, shuffling in the dry leaves, grunting, nocturnal animals; no danger.

Chapter Fifteen

The tent roof was translucent, wet parchment, spotted on the outside with early dew. Bird voices twirled over my ears, intricate as skaters or running water, the air filling with liquid syllables.

In the middle of the night there was a roar, Joe having a nightmare. I touched him, it was safe, he was trapped in the straitjacket sleeping bag. He sat up, not yet awake.

"This is the wrong room," he said.

"What was it?" I asked. "What were you dreaming?" I wanted to know, perhaps I could remember how. But he folded over and went back.

My hand was beside me; it had the cured hide smell of wood-smoke mingled with sweat and earth, fish lingering, smell of the past. At the cabin we would soak the clothes we'd been wearing, scrub the forest out of them, renew our coating of soap and lotion.

I dressed and went down to the lake and dipped my face into it. This water was not clear like the water in the main lake: it was brownish, complicated by more kinds of life crowded more closely together, and it was colder. The rock ledge dropped straight down, lake of the edge. I woke the others.

After I'd cleaned the fish I dipped them in flour and fried

them and boiled coffee. The fish flesh was white, blue-veined; it tasted like underwater and reeds. They ate, not talking much; they hadn't slept well.

Anna's face in the daylight was dried and slightly shrivelled without its cream underfilm and pink highlights; her nose was sunburned and she had prune crinkles under her eyes. She kept turned away from David, but he didn't seem to notice, he didn't say anything, except when she knocked her foot against his cup and tipped some of his coffee out onto the ground. Then all he said was "Watch it Anna, you're getting sloppy."

"Do you want to fish any more this morning?" I said to David, but he shook his head: "Let's go take that rock painting."

I burned the fish bones, the spines fragile as petals; the innards I planted in the forest. They were not seeds, in the spring no minnows would sprout up. Deer skeleton we found on the island, shreds of flesh on it still, he said the wolves had killed it in the winter because it was old, that was natural. If we dived for them and used our teeth to catch them, fighting on their own grounds, that would be fair, but hooks were substitutes and air wasn't their place.

The two of them fiddled with the movie camera, adjusting and discussing it; then we could start.

According to the map the rock painting was in a bay near the Americans' camp. They didn't seem to be up yet, there was no smoke coming from their fireplace. I thought, maybe it worked and they're dead.

I looked for a dip in the shore, a line that would fit the mapline. It was there, site of the x, unmistakable: cliff with sheer face, the kind they would have chosen to paint on, no other flat rock in sight. He had been here and long before him the original ones, the first explorers, leaving behind them their sign, word, but not its meaning. I leaned forward, scanning the cliff surface; we let the canoes drift in sideways till they scraped the stone.

"Where is it?" David said; and to Joe, "You'll have to steady the canoe, there's no way we can shoot from land."

"It might be hard to see at first," I said, "Faded. It ought to be right here somewhere." But it wasn't: no man with antlers, nothing like red paint or even a stain, the rock surface extended under my hand, coarse-grained, lunar, broken only by a pink-white vein of quartz that ran across it, a diagonal marking the slow tilt of the land; nothing human.

Either I hadn't remembered the map properly or what he'd written on the map was wrong. I'd reasoned it out, unravelled the clues in his puzzle the way he taught us and they'd led nowhere. I felt as though he'd lied to me.

"Who told you about it?" David said, cross-examining.

"I just thought it was here," I said. "Someone mentioned it. Maybe it was another lake." For a moment I knew: of course, the lake had been flooded, it would be twenty feet under water. But that was the other lake, this one was part of a separate system, the watershed divided them. The map said he'd found them on the main lake too; according to the letter he'd been taking pictures of them. But when I'd searched the cabin there had been no camera. No drawings, no camera, I'd done it wrong, I would have to look again.

They were disappointed, they'd expected something picturesque or bizarre, something they could utilize. He hadn't followed the rules, he'd cheated, I wanted to confront him, demand an explanation: You said it would be here.

We turned back. The Americans were up, they were still alive; they were setting out in their canoe, the front one had his fishing rod trailing over the bow. Joe and I were ahead, we approached them at right angles.

"Hi," the front one said, to me, bleached grin. "Any luck?" That was their armour, bland ignorance, heads empty as weather balloons: with that they could defend themselves against anything. Straight power, they mainlined it; I imagined the surge of electricity, nerve juice, as they hit it, brought it down, flapping like a crippled plane. The innocents get slaughtered because they exist, I thought, there is nothing inside the happy killers to restrain them, no conscience or piety; for them the only things worthy of life were human, their own kind of human, framed in the proper clothes and gimmicks, laminated. It would have been different in those countries where an animal is the soul of an ancestor or the child of a god, at least they would have felt guilt.

"We aren't fishing," I said, my lips clipping the words. My arm wanted to swing the paddle sideways, blade into his head: his eyes would blossom outwards, his skull shatter like an egg.

The corners of his mouth wilted. "Oh," he said. "Say, what part of the States are you all from? It's hard to tell, from your accent. Fred and me guessed Ohio."

"We're not from the States," I said, annoyed that he'd mistaken me for one of them.

"No kidding?" His face lit up, he'd seen a real native. "You from here?"

"Yes," I said. "We all are."

"So are we," said the back one unexpectedly.

The front one held out his hand, though five feet of water separated us. "I'm from Sarnia and Fred here, my brother-in-law, is from Toronto. We thought you were Yanks, with the hair and all."

I was furious with them, they'd disguised themselves. "What're you doing with that flag on your boat then?" I said, my voice loud, it surprised them. The front one withdrew his hand.

"Oh that," he said with a shrug. "I'm a Mets fan, have been for years, I always root for the underdog. Bought that when I was down there for the game, the year they won the pennant." I looked more closely at the sticker: it wasn't a flag at all, it was a blue and white oblong with red printing, GO METS.

David and Anna had caught up with us. "You a Mets fan?" David said. "Out of sight." He slid his canoe in beside theirs and they shook hands.

But they'd killed the heron anyway. It doesn't matter what country they're from, my head said, they're still Americans, they're what's in store for us, what we are turning into. They spread themselves like a virus, they get into the brain and take over the cells and the cells change from inside and the ones that have the disease can't tell the difference. Like the late show sci-fi movies, creatures from outer space, body snatchers injecting themselves into you dispossessing your brain, their eyes blank eggshells behind the dark glasses. If you look like them and talk like them and think like them then you are them, I was saying, you speak their language, a language is everything you do.

But how did they evolve, where did the first one come from, they weren't an invasion from another planet, they were terrestrial. How did we get bad. For us when we were small the origin was Hitler, he was the great evil, many-tentacled, ancient and indestructible as the Devil. It didn't matter that he had shrunk to a few cinders and teeth by the time I heard about him; I was certain he was alive, he was in the comic books my brother brought home in the winters and he was in my brother's scrapbook too, he was the swastikas on the tanks, if only he could be destroyed everyone would be saved, safe. When our father made bonfires to burn the weeds we would throw sticks into the flames and chant "Hitler's house is burning down, My Fair Lady-O"; we knew it helped. All possible horrors were measured against him. But Hitler was gone and the thing remained; whatever it was, even then, moving away from them as they smirked and waved goodbye, I was asking Are the Americans worse than Hitler. It was like cutting up a tapeworm, the pieces grew.

We landed at the campsite and rolled up the sleeping bags and struck the tents and packed them. I covered the toilet hole and smoothed it, camouflaging it with sticks and needles. Leave no traces.

David wanted to stay and have lunch with the Americans and talk about baseball scores, but I said the wind was against us, we would need the time. I hurried them, I wanted to get away, from my own anger as well as from the friendly metal killers.

We reached the first portage at eleven. My feet moved over the rocks and mud, stepping in my own day-old footprints, backtracking; in my brain the filaments, trails reconnected and branched, we killed other people besides Hitler, before my brother went to school and learned about him and the games became war games. Earlier we would play we were animals; our parents were the humans, the enemies who might shoot us or catch us, we would hide from them. But sometimes the animals had power too: one time we were a swarm of bees, we gnawed the fingers, feet and nose off our least favourite doll, ripped her cloth body open and pulled out the stuffing, it was grey and fluffy like the insides of mattresses; then we threw her into the lake. She floated and they found the body and asked us how she got lost, and we lied and said we didn't know. Killing was wrong, we had been told that: only enemies and food could be killed. Of course the doll wasn't hurt, it wasn't alive; though children think everything is alive.

At the midway pond the heron was still there, hanging in the hot sunlight like something in a butcher's window, desecrated, unredeemed. It smelled worse. Around its head the flies vibrated, laying their eggs. The king who learned to speak with animals, in the story he ate a magic leaf and they revealed a treasure, a conspiracy, they saved his life; what would they really say? Accusation, lament, an outcry of rage; but they had no spokesman.

I felt a sickening complicity, sticky as glue, blood on my hands, as though I had been there and watched without saying No or doing anything to stop it: one of the silent guarded faces in the crowd. The trouble some people have being German, I thought, I have being human. In a way it was stupid to be more disturbed by a dead bird than by those other things, the wars and riots and the massacres in the newspapers. But for the wars and riots there was always an explanation, people wrote books about them saying why they happened: the death of the heron was causeless, undiluted.

The laboratory, he was older then. He never caught birds, they were too quick for him, what he caught was the slower things. He kept them in jars and tin cans on a board shelf back in the forest, near the swamp; to reach them he made a secret path, marked only by small notches on the trees, a code. Sometimes he forgot to feed them or perhaps it was too cold at night, because when I went there by myself that day one of the snakes was dead and several of the frogs, their skin dry and their yellow stomachs puffed up, and the crayfish was floating in the clouded water with its legs uppermost like a spider's. I emptied those bottles into the swamp. The other things, the ones still alive, I let out. I rinsed the jars and tins and left them in a row on the board.

After lunch I hid but I had to come out finally for dinner. He couldn't say anything in front of them but he knew it was me, there was no one else. He was so angry he was pale, his eyes twisted as though they couldn't see me. "They were mine," he said. Afterwards he trapped other things and changed the place; this time he wouldn't tell me. I found it anyway but I was afraid to let them out again. Because of my fear they were killed.

I didn't want there to be wars and death, I wanted them not to exist; only rabbits with their coloured egg houses, sun and moon orderly above the flat earth, summer always, I wanted everyone to be happy. But his pictures were more accurate, the weapons, the disintegrating soldiers: he was a realist, that protected him. He almost drowned once but he would never allow that to happen again, by the time he left he was ready.

The leeches were there again in the tepid pond water, clumps of young ones hanging from the lily pad stems like fingers, larger ones swimming, flat and soft as noodles. I didn't like them but distaste excused nothing. In the other lake they never bothered us when we were swimming but we would catch the mottled kind, the bad kind he called them, and throw them on the campfire when our mother wasn't watching, she prohibited cruelty. I didn't mind that so much, if only they would die; but they would writhe out and crawl painfully, coated with ashes and pine needles, back towards the lake, seeming to be able to smell where the water was. Then he would pick them up with two sticks and put them back in the flames again.

It wasn't the city that was wrong, the inquisitors in the schoolyard, we weren't better than they were; we just had different victims. To become like a little child again, a barbarian, a vandal: it was in us too, it was innate. A thing closed in my head, hand, synapse, cutting off my escape: that was the wrong way, the entrance, redemption was elsewhere, I must have overlooked it.

We reached the main lake and re-loaded the canoes and shoved them out over the snarl of logs. In the bay the felled trees and numbered posts showed where the surveyors had been, power company. My country, sold or drowned, a reservoir; the people were sold along with the land and the animals, a bargain, sale, *solde*. Les soldes they called them, sellouts, the flood would depend on who got elected, not here but somewhere else.

Chapter Sixteen

It was the sixth day, I had to find out; it would be my last chance, tomorrow Evans was coming to take us back. My brain was rushing, covering over the bad things and filling the empty spaces with an embroidery of calculations and numbers, I needed to finish, I had never finished anything. To be exact, to condense myself to a pinpoint, impaling a fact, a certainty.

As soon as I could I re-checked the map. The x was where it should have been, I hadn't made a mistake. There was only one theory I could retreat to: some of the crosses might be places he thought suitable for paintings but hadn't examined yet. I ran my finger around the shore, looking for the nearest marked site; it was the cliff where we had been fishing the first evening, it would be underwater, I would have to dive. If I found something it would vindicate him, I would know he'd been right; if not I could try the next x, near the heron island, and then the next one.

I had my bathing suit on already; we'd been washing the clothes down on the dock, rubbing them on the ribbed washboard with the worn-down bar of yellow soap, standing in the lake to rinse them. They were pegged out to dry now on the line behind the cabin, shirts, jeans, socks, Anna's coloured lingerie, our cast skins. Anna had seemed more relaxed, she hummed from behind her fresh facade of makeup. She had stayed down by the lake to shampoo the smoke out of her hair. I pulled on a sweat shirt in case there were Americans. Before leaving I searched once more for his camera, the one he must have used to take the photographs, but it wasn't there; he must have had it with him. At the time, the last time.

I had started down the steps before I saw them. The three of them were on the dock, split into parts by the treetrunk bars. Anna was kneeling in her orange bikini, with a towel draped over her head like a nun; David was standing over her, hands on hips. Joe was further back with the movie camera, sitting on the dock with his legs dangling, head averted as if waiting politely for them to be through. When I heard what they were saying I stood still. The canoes were there and I needed one of them but it was too dangerous. It was a calm day, the sound carried.

"Come on, take it off," David said; his light-humour voice.

"I wasn't bothering you." Anna was muted, avoiding.

"It won't hurt you, we need a naked lady."

"What the hell for?" Anna was peevish now, her veiled head upturned; her eyes would be squinting.

"*Random Samples*," David said patiently, and I thought, They've used up everything, there's nothing left here now for them to take pictures of except each other, next it will be me. "You'll go in beside the dead bird, it's your chance for stardom, you've always wanted fame. You'll get to be on Educational T.V." he added as though it was a special bribe.

"Oh for Christ's sake," Anna said. She picked up her murder mystery again and pretended to read.

"Come on, we need a naked lady with big tits and a big ass," David said in the same tender voice; I recognized that menacing gentleness, at school it always went before the trick, the punchline.

"Look, will you leave me alone?" Anna said. "I'm minding my own business, mind yours why don't you." She stood up, her towel sliding off, and tried to get past him to the land, but he sidestepped in front of her.

"I won't take her if she doesn't want to," Joe said.

"It's token resistance," David said, "she wants to, she's an exhibitionist at heart. She likes her lush bod, don't you? Even if she is getting too fat."

"Don't think I don't know what you're trying to do," Anna said, as though she'd guessed a riddle. "You're trying to humiliate me."

"What's humiliating about your body, darling?" David said caressingly. "We all love it, you ashamed of it? That's pretty stingy of you, you should share the wealth; not that you don't."

Anna was furious now, goaded, her voice rose. "Fuck off, you want bloody everything don't you, you can't use that stuff on me."

"Why not," David said evenly, "it works. Now just take it off like a good girl or I'll have to take it off for you."

'Leave her alone," Joe said, swinging his legs, bored or excited, it was impossible to tell.

I wanted to run down to the dock and stop them, fighting was wrong, we weren't allowed to, if we did both sides got punished as in a real war. So we battled in secret, undeclared, and after a while I no longer fought back because I never won. The only defence was flight, invisibility. I sat down on the top step.

"Shut up, she's my wife," David said. His hand clamped down above her elbow. She jerked away, then I saw his arms go around her as if to kiss her and she was in the air, upside down over his shoulder, hair hanging in damp ropes. "Okay twatface," he said, "is it off or into the lake?"

Anna's fists grabbed bunches of his shirt. "If I go in, you go in too." The words spurted from behind her fallen hair, she was kicking, I couldn't see whether she was laughing or crying.

"Shoot," David said to Joe, and to Anna, "I'll count to ten."

Joe swivelled the camera and trained it on them like a

bazooka or a strange instrument of torture and pressed the button, lever, sinister whirr.

"All right," Anna said under its coercion, "you shmuck bastard, God damn you." He set her down and stepped aside. Her arms, elbows out, struggled with the fastener like a beetle's on its back and the top dropped away: I saw her cut in half, one breast on either side of a thin tree.

"Bottoms too," David said as though to a recalcitrant child. Anna glanced at him, contemptuous, and bent. "Look sexy now, move it; give us a little dance."

Anna stood for a moment, brown-red with yellow fur and white markings like underwear, glaring at them. Then she stuck her middle finger in the air at them and ran to the end of the dock and jumped into the lake. It was a bellyflop, the water splattered out like a dropped egg. She came up with her hair in streaks over her forehead and started to swim around towards the sand point, clumsy, arms flailing.

"Get that?" David said mildly over his shoulder.

"Some of it," Joe said. "Maybe you could order her to do it again." I thought he was being sarcastic but I wasn't sure. He began to unscrew the camera from the tripod.

I could hear Anna splashing and then stumbling below on the sand point; she was really crying now, her indrawn breaths rasping. The bushes rustled, she swore; then she appeared over the top of the hill, she must have climbed up by holding on to the leaning trees. Her pink face was dissolving, her skin was covered with sand and pine needles like a burned leech. She went into the cabin without looking at me or saying anything.

I stood up. Joe was gone but David was still on the dock, sitting now crosslegged. One at a time they were safer; I went down for the canoe.

"Hi," he said, "how goes it?" He didn't know I'd been watching. He had his shoes off and was picking at a toenail as though nothing had happened.

David is like me, I thought, we are the ones that don't

know how to love, there is something essential missing in us, we were born that way, Madame at the store with one hand, atrophy of the heart. Joe and Anna are lucky, they do it badly and suffer because of it: but it's better to see than to be blind, even though that way you had to let in the crimes and atrocities too. Or perhaps we are normal and the ones who can love are freaks, they have an extra organ, like the vestigial eye in the foreheads of amphibians they've never found the use for.

Anna's bikini lay on the dock, crumpled, a shed chrysalis. He picked up the top and began pleating and unpleating the strap. I hadn't meant to say anything about it, it wasn't my concern, but I found myself asking him anyway. "Why did you do that?" My voice was neutral and I realized it wasn't for Anna I was asking, I wasn't defending her; it was for myself, I needed to understand.

For a moment he acted. "What?" he said, grinning and innocent.

"What you just did to her."

He looked hard at me to see if I was accusing him but I was untying the canoe, I was impersonal as a wall, a confessional, and that reassured him. "You don't know what she does to me," he said with a slight whine. "She asks for it, she makes me do it." His voice turned crafty. "She goes with other men, she thinks she can get away with it, but she's too dumb, every time I find out; I can smell it on her. Not that I'd mind if she'd do it openly and be honest about it, God knows, it's not that I'm jealous." He smiled broadmindedly. "But she's devious, I can't stand that."

Anna hadn't told me, she had left something out; or else he was lying. "But she loves you," I said.

"Bullshit," he said "she's trying to cut my balls off." His eyes were sad rather than hostile, as though he had once believed better of her.

"She loves you," I repeated, petals off a daisy; it was the magic word but it couldn't work because I had no faith. My husband, saying it over and over like a Dial the Weather recording, trying to engrave it on me; and with the same bewilderment, as though I was the one who'd been hurting him and not the other way round. An accident, that's what he called it.

"She never tells *me* that," he said. "I get the impression she wants out, she's waiting for the chance to leave. But I haven't asked, we don't talk much any more except with other people around."

"Maybe you should," I said; unconvinced, unconvincing.

He shrugged. "What would we talk about? She's too dumb, she can't figure out what I'm saying to her, Jesus, she moves her lips when she watches the T.V. even. She doesn't know anything, every time she opens her mouth she makes an ass of herself. I know what you're thinking," he said, almost pleading, "but I'm all for the equality of women; she just doesn't happen to be equal and that's not my fault, is it? What I married was a pair of boobs, she manipulated me into it, it was when I was studying for the ministry, nobody knew any better then. But that's life." He wiggled his moustache and gave a Woody Woodpecker laugh, his eyes baffled.

"I think you could work it out," I said. I braced the paddle across the gunwhales and clambered into the canoe. I remembered what Anna had said about emotional commitments: they've made one, I thought, they hate each other; that must be almost as absorbing as love. The barometer couple in their wooden house, enshrined in their niche on Paul's front porch, my ideal; except they were glued there, condemned to oscillate back and forth, sun and rain, without escape. When he saw her next there would be no recantations, no elaborate reconciliation or forgiveness, they were beyond that. Neither of them would mention it, they had reached a balance almost like peace. Our mother and father at the sawhorse behind the cabin, mother holding the tree, white birch, father sawing, sun through the branches lighting their hair, grace.

The canoe pivoted. "Hey," he said, "where you off to?"

"Oh. . . ." I gestured towards the lake.

"Want a stern paddler?" he said. "I'm great, I've had lots of practice by now."

He sounded wistful, as though he needed company, but I didn't want him with me, I'd have to explain what I was doing and he wouldn't be able to help. "No," I said, "thanks just the same." I knelt, slanting the canoe to one side.

"Okay," he said, "see you later, alligator." He unwound his legs and stood up and strolled off the dock towards the cabin, his striped T-shirt flashing between the slats of the trees, receding behind me as I glided from the bay into the open water.

Chapter Seventeen

I moved toward the cliff. The sun sloped, it was morning still, the light not yellow but clear white. Overhead a plane, so far up I could hardly hear it, threading the cities together with its trail of smoke; an x in the sky, unsacred crucifix. The shape of the heron flying above us the first evening we fished, legs and neck stretched, wings outspread, a bluegrey cross, and the other heron or was it the same one, hanging wrecked from the tree. Whether it died willingly, consented, whether Christ died willingly, anything that suffers and dies instead of us is Christ; if they didn't kill birds and fish they would have killed us. The animals die that we may live, they are substitute people, hunters in the fall killing the deer, that is Christ also. And we eat them, out of cans or otherwise; we are eaters of death, dead Christ-flesh resurrecting inside us, granting us life. Canned Spam, canned Jesus, even the plants must be Christ. But we refuse to worship; the body worships with blood and muscle but the thing in the knob head will not, wills not to, the head is greedy, it consumes but does not give thanks.

I reached the cliff, there were no Americans. I edged along it, estimating the best place to dive: it faced east, the sun was on it, it was the right time of day; I would start at the left-hand side. Diving by myself was hazardous, there ought to be another person. But I thought I remembered how: we took the canoes or we built rafts from strayed logs and board ends, they would often snap their ropes and escape in the spring when the ice went out; sometimes we would come across them again later, drifting loose like pieces broken from a glacier.

I shipped the paddle and took off my sweatshirt. I would dive several feet out from the rockface and then swim down and in: otherwise I'd risk hitting my head, the drop looked sheer but there might be a ledge underwater. I knelt, facing backwards with both knees on the stern seat, then put a foot on each gunwale and stood up slowly. I bent my knees and straightened, the canoe teetered like a springboard. My other shape was in the water, not my reflection but my shadow, foreshortened, outline blurred, rays streaming out from around the head.

My spine whipped, I hit the water and kicked myself down, sliding through the lake strata, grey to darker grey, cool to cold. I arched sideways and the rockface loomed up, grey pink brown; I worked along it, touching it with my fingers, snail touch on slimesurface, the water unfocusing my eyes. Then my lungs began to clutch and I curled and rose, letting out air like a frog, my hair swirling over my face, towards the canoe, where it hung split between water and air, mediator and liferaft. I canted it with my weight and rolled into it over the side and rested; I hadn't seen anything. My arms ached from the day before and the new effort, my body stumbled, it remembered the motions only imperfectly, like learning to walk after illness.

I waited a few minutes, then moved the canoe further along and dived again, my eyes straining, not knowing what shape to expect, handprint or animal, the lizard body with horns and tail and front-facing head, bird or canoe with stick paddlers; or a small thing, an abstraction, a circle, a moon; or a long distorted figure, stiff and childish, a human. Air gave out, I broke surface. Not here, it must be further along or deeper down; I was convinced it was there, he would not have marked and numbered the map so methodically for nothing, that would not be consistent, he always observed his own rules, axioms.

On the next try I thought I saw it, a bloth, a shadow, just as I turned to go up. I was dizzy, my vision was beginning to cloud, while I rested my ribs panted, I ought to pause, half an hour at least; but I was elated, it was down there, I would find it. Reckless I balanced and plunged.

Pale green, then darkness, layer after layer, deeper than before, seabottom; the water seemed to have thickened, in it pinprick lights flicked and darted, red and blue, yellow and white, and I saw they were fish, the chasm-dwellers, fins lined with phosphorescent sparks, teeth neon. It was wonderful that I was down so far, I watched the fish, they swam like patterns on closed eyes, my legs and arms were weightless, free-floating; I almost forgot to look for the cliff and the shape.

It was there but it wasn't a painting, it wasn't on the rock. It was below me, drifting towards me from the furthest level where there was no life, a dark oval trailing limbs. It was blurred but it had eyes, they were open, it was something I knew about, a dead thing, it was dead.

I turned, fear gushing out of my mouth in silver, panic closing my throat, the scream kept in and choking me. The green canoe was far above me, sunlight radiating around it, a beacon, safety.

But there was not one canoe, there were two, the canoe had twinned or I was seeing double. My hand came out of the water and I gripped the gunwale, then my head; water ran from my nose, I gulped breath, stomach and lungs contracting, my hair sticky like weeds, the lake was horrible, it was filled with death, it was touching me.

Joe was in the other canoe. "He told me you went over this way," he said. He must have been almost there before I dived but I hadn't seen him. I couldn't say anything, my lungs were urgent, my arms would hardly pull me into the canoe.

"What the hell are you doing?" he said.

I lay on the bottom of the canoe and closed my eyes; I wanted him not to be there. It formed again in my head: at first I thought it was my drowned brother, hair floating around the face, image I'd kept from before I was born; but it couldn't be him, he had not drowned after all, he was elsewhere. Then I recognized it: it wasn't ever my brother I'd been remembering, that had been a disguise.

I knew when it was, it was in a bottle curled up, staring out at me like a cat pickled; it had huge jelly eyes and fins instead of hands, fish gills, I couldn't let it out, it was dead already, it had drowned in air. It was there when I woke up, suspended in the air above me like a chalice, an evil grail and I thought, Whatever it is, part of myself or a separate creature, I killed it. It wasn't a child but it could have been one, I didn't allow it.

Water was dripping from me into the canoe, I lay in a puddle. I had been furious with them, I knocked it off the table, my life on the floor, glass egg and shattered blood, nothing could be done.

That was wrong, I never saw it. They scraped it into a bucket and threw it wherever they throw them, it was travelling through the sewers by the time I woke, back to the sea, I stretched my hand up to it and it vanished. The bottle had been logical, pure logic, remnant of the trapped and decaying animals, secreted by my head, enclosure, something to keep the death away from me. Not even a hospital, not even that sanction of legality, official procedures. A house it was, shabby front room with magazines, purple runner on the hall floor, vines and blossoms, the smell of lemon polish, furtive doors and whispers, they wanted you out fast. Pretense of the non-nurse, her armpits acid, face powdered with solicitude. Stumble along the hall, from flower to flower, her criminal hand on my elbow, other arm against the wall. Ring on my finger. It was all real enough, it was enough reality for ever, I couldn't accept it, that mutilation, ruin I'd made, I needed a different version. I pieced it together the best way I could, flattening it, scrapbook, collage, pasting over the wrong parts. A faked album, the memories fraudulent as passports; but a paper house was better than none and I could almost live in it, I'd lived in it until now.

He hadn't gone with me to the place where they did it; his own children, the real ones, were having a birthday party. But he came afterwards to collect me. It was a hot day, when we stepped out into the sun we couldn't see for an instant. It wasn't a wedding, there were no pigeons, the post office and the lawn were in another part of the city where I went for stamps; the fountain with the dolphins and the cherub with half a face was from the company town, I'd put it in so there would be something of mine.

"It's over," he said, "feel better?"

I was emptied, amputated; I stank of salt and antiseptic, they had planted death in me like a seed.

"You're cold," he said, "come on, we'd better get you home." Scrutinizing my face in the light, hands on the wheel, tough, better this way. In my deflated lap there was a purse, suitcase. I couldn't go there, home, I never went there again, I sent them a postcard.

They never knew, about that or why I left. Their own innocence, the reason I couldn't tell them; perilous innocence, closing them in glass, their artificial garden, greenhouse. They didn't teach us about evil, they didn't understand about it, how could I describe it to them? They were from another age, prehistoric, when everyone got married and had a family, children growing in the yard like sunflowers; remote as Eskimoes or mastodons.

I opened my eyes and sat up. Joe was still there beside me; he was holding on to the edge of my canoe.

"You all right?" he said. His voice came to me faintly, as though muffled.

He said I should do it, he made me do it; he talked about it as though it was legal, simple, like getting a wart removed. He said it wasn't a person, only an animal; I should have seen that was no different, it was hiding in me as if in a burrow and instead of granting it sanctuary I let them catch it. I could have said no but I didn't; that made me one of them too, a killer. After the slaughter, the murder, he couldn't believe I didn't want to see him any more; it bewildered him, he resented me for it, he expected gratitude because he arranged it for me, fixed me so I was as good as new; others, he said, wouldn't have bothered. Since then I'd carried that death around inside me, layering it over, a cyst, a tumour, black pearl; the gratitude I felt now was not for him.

I had to go onto the shore and leave something: that was what you were supposed to do, leave a piece of your clothing as an offering. I regretted the nickels I'd taken dutifully for the collection plate, I got so little in return: no power remained in their bland oleotinted Jesus prints or in the statues of the other ones, rigid and stylized, holy triple name shrunken to swearwords. These gods, here on the shore or in the water, unacknowledged or forgotten, were the only ones who had ever given me anything I needed; and freely.

The map crosses and the drawings made sense now: at the beginning he must have been only locating the rock paintings, deducing them, tracing and photographing them, a retirement hobby; but then he found out about them. The Indians did not own salvation but they had once known where it lived and their signs marked the sacred places, the places where you could learn the truth. There was no painting at White Birch Lake and none here, because his later drawings weren't copied from things on the rocks. He had discovered new places, new oracles, they were things he was seeing the way I had seen, true vision; at the end, after the failure of logic. When it happened the first time he must have been terrified, it would be like stepping through a usual door and finding yourself in a different galaxy, purple trees and red moons and a green sun.

I swung the paddle and Joe's hand came unstuck and the canoe went towards the shore. I slipped on my canvas shoes and bundled up the sweatshirt and stepped out, looping the rope to a tree, then I climbed the slope towards the cliff, trees on one side, rockface on the other, balsam smell, underbrush scratching my bare legs. There was a ledge, I'd noticed it from the lake, I could throw my sweatshirt onto it. I didn't know the names of the ones I was making the offering to; but they were there, they had power. Candles in front of statues, crutches on the steps, flowers in jam jars by the roadside crosses, gratitude for cures, however wished-for and partial. Clothing was better, it was closer and more essential; and the gift had been greater, more than a hand or an eye, feeling was beginning to seep back into me, I tingled like a foot that's been asleep.

I was opposite the ledge; reindeer moss feathered it, clumps intricate with branches, the tips red, glowing in the sun. It was only an arm's length away on the sheer cliff; I folded my sweatshirt neatly and reached it across.

Behind me something lumbered, crashing. It was Joe, I'd forgotten about him. When he caught up with me he took me by the shoulders.

"You all right?" he said again.

I didn't love him, I was far away from him, it was as though I was seeing him through a smeared window or glossy paper; he didn't belong here. But he existed, he deserved to be alive. I was wishing I could tell him how to change so he could get there, the place where I was.

"Yes," I said. I touched him on the arm with my hand. My hand touched his arm. Hand touched arm. Language divides us into fragments, I wanted to be whole.

He kissed me; I stood on my side of the window. When his head drew away I said "I don't love you," I was going to explain but he didn't seem to hear me, mouth on my shoulder, fingers at the clasp behind my back, then sliding down my flanks, he was pushing on me as though trying to fold up a lawn chair, he wanted me to lie down on the ground.

I stretched out inside my body, twigs and pine needles under me. At that moment I thought, Perhaps for him I am the entrance, as the lake was the entrance for me. The forest condensed in him, it was noon, the sun was behind his head; his face was invisible, the sun's rays coming out from a centre of darkness, my shadow.

His hands descended, zipper sound, metal teeth on metal teeth, he was rising out of the fur husk, solid and heavy; but the cloth separated from him and I saw he was human, I didn't want him in me, sacrilege, he was one of the killers, the clay victims damaged and strewn behind him, and he hadn't seen, he didn't know about himself, his own capacity for death.

"Don't," I said, he was lowering himself down on me, "I don't want you to."

"What's wrong with you?" he said, angry; then he was pinning me, hands manacles, teeth against my lips, censoring me, he was shoving against me, his body insistent as one side of an argument.

I slid my arm between us, against his throat, windpipe, and pried his head away. "I'll get pregnant," I said, "it's the right time." It was the truth, it stopped him: flesh making more flesh, miracle, that frightens all of them.

He reached the dock first, outdistancing me, his fury propelling the canoe like a motor. By the time I got there he had vanished.

Chapter Eighteen

There was no one in the cabin. It was different, larger, as though I hadn't been there for a long time: the half of me that had begun to return was not yet used to it. I went back outside and unhooked the gate of the fenced oblong and sat down on the swing, carefully, the ropes still held my weight; I swayed myself gently back and forth, keeping my feet on the ground. Rocks, trees, sandbox where I made houses with stones for windows. The birds were there, chickadees and jays; but they were wary of me, they weren't trained.

I turned the ring on my left-hand finger, souvenir: he gave it to me, plain gold, he said he didn't like ostentation, it got us into the motels easier, opener of doors; in the intervening time I wore it on a chain around my neck. The cold bathrooms, interchangeable, feel of tile on footsoles, walking into them wrapped in someone else's towel in the days of rubber sex, precautions. He would prop his watch on the nighttables to be sure he wasn't late.

For him I could have been anyone but for me he was unique, the first, that's where I learned. I worshipped him, non-child-bride, idolater, I kept the scraps of his handwriting like saints' relics, he never wrote letters, all I had was the criticisms in red pencil he paperclipped to my drawings. cs and ds, he was an idealist, he said he didn't want our relationship as he called it to influence his aesthetic judgment. He didn't want our relationship to influence anything; it was to be kept separate from life. A certificate framed on the wall, his proof that he was still young.

He did say he loved me though, that part was true; I didn't make it up. It was the night I locked myself in and turned on the water in the bathtub and he cried on the other side of the door. When I gave up and came out he showed me snapshots of his wife and children, his reasons, his stuffed and mounted family, they had names, he said I should be mature.

I heard the thin dentist's-drill sound of a powerboat approaching, more Americans; I got off the swing and went halfway down the steps where I would be shielded by the trees. They slowed their motor and curved into the bay. I crouched and watched, at first I thought they were going to land: but they were only gazing, surveying, planning the attack and the takeover. They pointed up at the cabin and talked, flash of binoculars. Then they accelerated and headed off towards the cliff where the gods lived. But they wouldn't catch anything, they wouldn't be allowed. It was dangerous for them to go there without knowing about the power; they might hurt themselves, a false move, metal hooks lowered into the sacred water, that could touch it off like electricity or a grenade. I had endured it only because I had a talisman, my father had left me the guides, the man-animals and the maze of numbers.

It would be right for my mother to have left something for me also, a legacy. His was complicated, tangled, but hers would be simple as a hand, it would be final. I was not completed yet; there had to be a gift from each of them.

I wanted to search for it but David was jogging down the path from the outhouse. "Hi," he called, "you seen Anna?"

"No," I said. If I went back to the house or into the garden he would follow me and talk. I stood up and walked down the rest of the steps and ducked into the trail entrance through the long grass.

In the cool green among the trees, new trees and stumps,

the stumps with charcoal crusts on them, scabby and crippled, survivors of an old disaster. Sight flowing ahead of me over the ground, eyes filtering the shapes, the names of things fading but their forms and uses remaining, the animals learned what to eat without nouns. Six leaves, three leaves, the root of this is crisp. White stems curved like question marks, fish-coloured in the dim light, corpse plants, inedible. Finger-shaped yellow fungi, unclassified, I never memorized all of them; and further along a mushroom with cup and ring and chalk gills and a name: Death Angel, deadly poison. Beneath it the invisible part, threadlike underground network of which this was the solid flower, temporary as an icicle, growth frozen; tomorrow it would be melted but the roots would stay. If our bodies lived in the earth with only the hair sprouting up through the leafmould it would seem as if that was all we were, filament plants.

The reason they invented coffins, to lock the dead in, preserve them, they put makeup on them; they didn't want them spreading or changing into anything else. The stone with the name and the date was on them to weight them down. She would have hated it, that box, she would have tried to get out; I ought to have stolen her out of that room and brought her here and let her go away by herself into the forest, she would have died anyway but quicker, lucidly, not in that glass case.

It sprang up from the earth, pure joy, pure death, burning white like snow.

The dry leaves shuffled behind me: he had shadowed me along the trail. "Hi, whatcha doin'?" he said.

I didn't turn or speak but he didn't wait for an answer, he sat down beside me and said "What's that?"

I had to concentrate in order to talk to him, the English words seemed imported, foreign; it was like trying to listen to two separate conversations, each interrupting the other. "A mushroom," I said. That wouldn't be enough, he would want a specific term. My mouth jumped like a stutterer's and the Latin appeared. "Amanita."

"Neat," he said, but he wasn't interested. I willed him to go away but he didn't; after a while he put his hand on my knee.

"Well?" he said.

I looked at him. His smile was like a benevolent uncle's; under his forehead there was a plan, it corrugated the skin. I pushed his hand off and he put it back again.

"How about it?" he said. "You wanted me to follow you."

His fingers were squeezing, he was drawing away some of the power, I would lose it and come apart again, the lies would recapture. "Please don't," I said.

"Come on now, don't give me hassle," he said. "You're a groovy chick, you know the score, you aren't married." He reached his arm around me, invading, and pulled me over towards him; his neck was creased and freckled, soon he would have jowls, he smelled like scalp. His moustache whisked my face.

I twisted away and stood up. "Why are you doing this?" I said. "You're interfering." I wiped at my arm where he had touched it.

He didn't understand what I meant, he smiled even harder. "Don't get uptight," he said, "I won't tell Joe. It'll be great, it's good for you, keeps you healthy." Then he went "Yuk, yuk" like Goofy.

He was speaking about it as though it was an exercising programme, athletic demonstration, ornamental swimming in a chlorine swimming pool noplace in California. "It wouldn't keep me healthy," I said, "I'd get pregnant."

He lifted his eyebrows, incredulous. "You're putting me on," he said, "this is the twentieth century."

"No it isn't," I said. "Not here."

He stood up also and took a step towards me. I backed away. He was turning mottled pink, turkey neck, but his voice was still rational. "Listen," he said, "I realize you walk around in never-never land but don't tell me you don't know where Joe is; he's not so noble, he's off in the bushes somewhere with that cunt on four legs, right about now he's shoving it into her." He glanced quickly at his wristwatch as though timing them; he seemed elated by what he'd said, his eyes gleamed like test-tubes.

"Oh," I said; I thought about it for a minute. "Maybe they love each other." It would be logical, they were the ones who could. "Do you love me," I asked in case I hadn't understood him, "is that why you want me to?"

He thought I was being either smart or stupid and said "Christ." Then he paused, aiming. "You aren't going to let him get away with it, are you?" he said. "Tit for tat as they say." He folded his arms, resting his case, retaliation was his ultimate argument: he must have felt it was a duty, an obligation on my part, it would be justice. Geometrical sex, he needed me for an abstract principle; it would be enough for him if our genitals could be detached like two kitchen appliances and copulate in mid-air, that would complete his equation.

His wristwatch glittered, glass and silver: perhaps it was his dial, the key that wound him, the switch. There must be a phrase, a vocabulary that would work. "I'm sorry," I said, "but you don't turn me on."

"You," he said, searching for words, not controlled any more, "tight-ass bitch."

The power flowed into my eyes, I could see into him, he was an imposter, a pastiche, layers of political handbills, pages from magazines, *affiches*, verbs and nouns glued on to him and shredding away, the original surface littered with fragments and tatters. In a black suit knocking on doors, young once, even that had been a costume, a uniform; now his hair was falling off and he didn't know what language to use, he'd forgotten his own, he had to copy. Second-hand American was spreading over him in patches, like mange or lichen. He was infested, garbled, and I couldn't help him: it would take such time to heal, unearth him, scrape down to where he was true.

"Keep it to yourself then," he said, "I'm not going to sit up and beg for a little third-rate cold tail."

I detoured around past him, back towards the cabin. More than ever I needed to find it, the thing she had hidden; the power from my father's intercession wasn't enough to protect me, it gave only knowledge and there were more gods than his, his were the gods of the head, antlers rooted in the brain. Not only how to see but how to act.

I thought he would stay there, at least till I was out of range, but he followed along behind me. "Sorry I blew my cool," he said. His voice had changed again, now it was deferential. "It's between us, okay? No need to mention it to Anna, right?" If he'd succeeded he would have told her as soon as he could. "I respect you for it, I really do."

"That's all right," I said; I knew he was lying.

They sat around the table in the regular places and I served dinner. There hadn't been any lunch but no one mentioned that.

"What time is Evans coming tomorrow?" I said.

"Ten, ten-thirty," David said. "Have a nice afternoon?" he said to Anna. Joe stuck a new potato with his fork and put it into his mouth.

"Fantastic," Anna said. "I got some sun and finished my book, then I had a long talk with Joe and went for a stroll." Joe chewed, his closed mouth moving, silent refutation. "And you?"

"Great," David said, his voice buoyant, inflated. He bent his arm onto the table, his hand brushing mine casually, as though by accident, for her to see. I flinched away, he was lying about me, the animals don't lie.

Anna smiled mournfully at him. I watched him, he wasn't laughing, he was staring at her, the lines in his face deepening and sagging. They know everything about each other, I thought, that's why they're so sad; but Anna was more than sad, she was desperate, her body her only weapon and she was fighting for her life, he was her life, her life was the fight: she was fighting him because if she ever surrendered the balance

147

of power would be broken and he would go elsewhere. To continue the war.

I didn't want to join. "It's not what you think," I said to Anna. "He asked me to but I wouldn't." I wanted to tell her I hadn't acted against her.

Her eyes flicked from him to me. "That was pure of you," she said. I'd made a mistake, she resented me because I hadn't given in, it commented on her.

"She's pure all right," David said, "she's a little purist."

"Joe told me she won't put out for him any more," Anna said, still looking at me. Joe didn't say anything; he was eating another potato.

"She hates men," David said lightly. "Either that or she wants to be one. Right?"

A ring of eyes, tribunal; in a minute they would join hands and dance around me, and after that the rope and the pyre, cure for heresy.

Maybe it was true, I leafed through all the men I had known to see whether or not I hated them. But then I realized it wasn't the men I hated, it was the Americans, the human beings, men and women both. They'd had their chance but they had turned against the gods, and it was time for me to choose sides. I wanted there to be a machine that could make them vanish, a button I could press that would evaporate them without disturbing anything else, that way there would be more room for the animals, they would be rescued.

"Aren't you going to answer?" Anna said, taunting.

"No," I said.

Anna said, "God, she really is inhuman," and they both laughed a little, sorrowfully.

Chapter Nineteen

I cleared the table and scraped the canned ham fat scraps from the plates into the fire, food for the dead. If you fed them enough they would come back; or was it the reverse, if you fed them enough they would stay away, it was in one of the books but I'd forgotten.

Anna said she would wash the dishes. It was an apology perhaps, reparation for the fact that she'd found it easier to fight on his side than against him. For once. She rattled the cutlery in the pan, singing to avoid discussion, we were beyond the time for confidences; her voice occupied the room, territorial.

It had to be inside the house. Before supper I searched the toolshed, while I was getting the shovel, and the garden when I dug up the potatoes; but it wasn't there, I would have recognized it. It had to be something out of place, something that wasn't here when I left, apple in the row of oranges like the old arithmetic workbooks. She would have brought it here especially for me and hidden it where I would discover it when I was ready; like my father's puzzle it would mediate, we cannot approach them directly. I dried the dishes as Anna washed, inspecting each one to make sure it was familiar. But nothing had been added since I'd been here, the gift was not a dish.

It wasn't anywhere in the main room. When we'd finished

I went into David's and Anna's room: her leather jacket was there, hanging up, it hadn't been put back since the trip. I examined the pockets; there was nothing in them but an empty metal aspirin container and an ancient kleenex, and the husks from sunflower seeds; and a charred filter from one of Anna's cigarettes, which I dropped on the floor and crushed with my foot.

My room was the only one remaining. As soon as I stepped inside it I sensed the power, in my hands and running along my arms, I was close to it. I scanned the walls and shelves, it wasn't there; my painted ladies watched me with their bristling eyes. Then I was certain: it was in the scrapbooks, I'd shoved them under the mattress without reading through all of them. They were the last possibility and they weren't supposed to be here, they belonged in the city, in the trunk.

I heard a motor droning from down the lake, a different pitch, deeper than a powerboat.

"Hey look," Anna called from the main room, "A big boat!" We went out on the point: it was a police launch like the ones driven by the game wardens, they were checking us the way they used to, to see if we had any dead fish and a licence to go with them; it was routine.

The launch slowed and drew into the dock. David was down there anyway, I would let him meet it, he was the one with the papers. I re-entered the house and stood by the window. Anna, inquisitive, sauntered down to join them.

There were two men, police or probably game wardens, they were wearing ordinary clothes; and a third man, blond, Claude from the village probably, and a fourth one, older, the size of Paul. It was odd that Paul was on the launch: if he were coming for a visit he would bring his own boat. David shook hands with them and they clustered on the dock, talking in low voices. David dug into his pocket, for the licence; then he scratched his neck as if worried. Joe appeared from the outhouse path and the talking started over again; Anna's head turned up towards me.

Then I saw David hurrying, taking the hill steps two at a time. The screen door banged shut behind him. "They found your father," he said, breathing hard from the climb. He squinted his face, as if to show sympathy.

The door slammed again, it was Anna; he put his arm around her and they both studied me with the intent pouncing look they'd had at supper.

"Oh," I said. "Where?"

"Some American guys found him in the lake. They were fishing, they hooked him by mistake; the body was unrecognizable but an old guy named Paul something-or-other down there, says he knows you, he identified the clothes. They figured he'd fallen off a cliff or something, he had a skull fracture." Seedy department-store magician, producing my father out of nowhere like a stuffed rabbit out of a hat.

"Where?" I said again.

"It's awful," Anna said, "I'm really sorry."

"They don't know where it happened," David said, "he must've drifted; he had a camera around his neck, big one, they think the weight kept him down or he would've been found sooner." His eyes gloating.

It was clever of him to have guessed the missing camera, since I'd told them nothing. He must have thought quickly in order to make it all up in such a short time: I knew it was a lie, he was doing it to get back at me. "Did they ask to see your fishing licence?" I said.

"No," he said, faking surprise. "You want to talk to them?"

That was a risk, he should have calculated better, it would expose his whole false construction. Maybe that's what he wanted, maybe it was intended as a practical joke. I decided to act as though I believed him, see how he'd get out of it. "No," I said, "tell them I'm too upset. I'll speak to Paul tomorrow when we get to the village, about the arrangements." That was what they were called, the arrangements. "He'd want to be buried around here." Convincing details, if he could invent I could invent also, I'd read enough murder mysteries. The detectives, eccentric hermits, orchid-raisers, sharp bluehaired old ladies, girls with jackknives and flashlights, for them everything fitted. But not in real life, I wanted to tell him, you've outsmarted yourself.

He and Anna glanced at each other: they'd planned on hurting me. "Okay," he said.

Anna said, "Wouldn't you rather . . ." and then stopped. They walked back down the steps, disappointed both of them, their trap had failed.

I went into the other room and took the scrapbooks out from under the mattress. There was still enough light to see by but I closed my eyes, touching the covers with my hands, fingertips. One of them was heavier and warmer; I lifted it, let it fall open. My mother's gift was there for me, I could look.

The rest of the scrapbook had early people, hairs blazing out of their heads like rays or spikes, and suns with faces, but the gift itself was a loose page, the edge torn, the figures drawn in crayon. On the left was a woman with a round moon stomach: the baby was sitting up inside her gazing out. Opposite her was a man with horns on his head like cow horns and a barbed tail.

The picture was mine, I had made it. The baby was myself before I was born, the man was God, I'd drawn him when my brother learned in the winter about the Devil and God: if the Devil was allowed a tail and horns, God needed them also, they were advantages.

That was what the pictures had meant then but their first meaning was lost now like the meanings of the rock paintings. They were my guides, she had saved them for me, pictographs, I had to read their new meaning with the help of the power. The gods, their likenesses: to see them in their true shape is fatal. While you are human; but after the transformation they could be reached. First I had to immerse myself in the other language.

Launch vibration, going away. I slid the page back into the scrapbook and replaced it under the mattress. Trample of the others on the hill, I stayed inside the room.

They lit the lamp. Noise of David fumbling and then the cards, he was laying out a game of solitaire; then Anna's voice, she wanted to set up the other deck. They were playing doubles, slapping the cards down expertly as gamblers, mono-syllables as they gained or lost. Joe sat in the corner on the bench, I could hear him scuffling against the wall.

For him truth might still be possible, what will preserve him is the absence of words; but the others are already turn-ing to metal, skins galvanizing, heads congealing to brass knobs, components and intricate wires ripening inside. The cards tick on the table.

I unclose my fist, releasing, it becomes a hand again, palm a network of trails, lifeline, past present and future, the break in it closing together as I purse my fingers. When the heartline and the headline are one, Anna told us, you are either a crim-inal, an idiot or a saint. How to act.

Their voices murmur, they can't discuss me, they know I'm listening. They're avoiding me, they find me inappropri-ate; they think I should be filled with death, I should be in mourning. But nothing has died, everything is alive, every-thing is waiting to become alive.

THREE

Chapter Twenty

The sunset was red, a clear tulip colour paling to flesh webs, membrane. Now there are only streaks of it, mauve and purple, sky visible through the window, divided by the window squares and then by the interlacing branches, leaves overlapping leaves. I'm in the bed, covered up, clothes in a pile on the floor, he will be here soon, they can't postpone it forever.

Mumbles, cards gathered, swish and spit of teeth being brushed. Blown breath and guttering, the lamp goes out, the flashlight beams wash over the ceiling. He opens the door and stands hesitating, darkening the light he holds, after the morning and the afternoon he isn't sure how to approach me. I feign sleep and he feels his way into the room, stealthy as moss, and unzips his human skin.

He thinks I'm in pain, he wants to evade it, he bends himself away from me; but I stroke him, move my hand over his body, he's startled because I'm awake. After a minute he turns to me, stiffening, arms going around me and over me and I smell Anna on him, suntan lotion and pink face grease and smoke, but that doesn't matter; what matters is the other smell, smells, the sheets, wool and soap, chemically treated hides, I can't here. I sit up, swing my legs out of the bed.

"Now what?" he says, whispers.

I tug at his hands. "Not here."

"Christl!" He tries to pull me back down but I brace my legs, hooking them onto the side.

"Don't talk," I say.

He stumbles out of the bed then and follows me, from this room to the other and across the outer floor. When I've unlatched the screen door and the wooden door I take his hand: there is something outside which I have protection against but he doesn't, I have to keep him close to me, inside the radius.

We go over the ground, feet and skin bare; the moon is rising, in the greygreen light his body gleams and the trunks of trees, the white ovals of his eyes. He walks as though blind, blundering into the shadow clumps, toes stubbing, he has not yet learned to see in the dark. My tentacled feet and free hand scent out the way, shoes are a barrier between touch and the earth. Double thump, clutched heartbeat: rabbits, warning us and each other. On the far shore an owl, its voice feathered and clawed, black on black, blood in the heart.

I lie down, keeping the moon on my left hand and the absent sun on my right. He kneels, he is shivering, the leaves under and around us are damp from the dew, or is it the lake, soaking up through the rock and sand, we are near the shore, the small waves riffle. He needs to grow more fur.

"What is it?" he says. "What's wrong?" My hands are on his shoulders, he is thick, undefined, outline but no features, hair and beard a mane, moon behind him. He turns to curve over me; his eyes glint, he is shaking, fear or tensed flesh or the cold. I pull him down, his beard and hair fall over me like ferns, mouth as soft as water. Heavy on me, warm stone, almost alive.

"I love you," he says into the side of my neck, catechism. Teeth grinding, he's holding back, he wants it to be like the city, baroque scrollwork, intricate as a computer, but I'm impatient, pleasure is redundant, the animals don't have pleasure. I guide him into me, it's the right season, I hurry.

He trembles and then I can feel my lost child surfacing

within me, forgiving me, rising from the lake where it has been prisoned for so long, its eyes and teeth phosphorescent; the two halves clasp, interlocking like fingers, it buds, it sends out fronds. This time I will do it by myself, squatting, on old newspapers in a corner alone; or on leaves, dry leaves, a heap of them, that's cleaner. The baby will slip out easily as an egg, a kitten, and I'll lick it off and bite the cord, the blood returning to the ground where it belongs; the moon will be full, pulling. In the morning I will be able to see it: it will be covered with shining fur, a god, I will never teach it any words.

I press my arms around him, smoothing his back; I'm grateful to him, he's given me the part of himself I needed. I'll take him back to the cabin, through the force that presses in on us now like deepsea on a diver, then I can let him go.

"Is it all right?" he says. He's lying on top of me, breathing, molten. "Was it all right?"

He means two different things; but "Yes" I say, answer to a third question, unasked. Nobody must find out or they will do that to me again, strap me to the death machine, emptiness machine, legs in the metal framework, secret knives. This time I won't let them.

"Then it's okay," he says; he's leaning on his elbows, with his fingers and lips he soothes me, my cheek, hair. "It wasn't anything this afternoon, it didn't mean anything; it was her that wanted it." He rolls off me, lies beside me, nuzzling against my shoulder for warmth; he's shivering again. "Shit," he says, "it's bloody freezing." Then, cautiously, "Now do you?"

It's love, the ritual word, he wants to know again; but I can't give redemption, even as a lie. We both wait for my answer. The wind moves, rustling of tree lungs, water lapping all around us.

Chapter Twenty-One

When I wake up it's morning, we're in the bed again. He is awake already, head hovering above me, he was surveying me while I slept. He smiles, a plump smile, contented, his beard puffed up like a singing toad throat, and lowers his face to kiss me. He still doesn't understand, he thinks he has won, act of his flesh a rope noosed around my neck, leash, he will lead me back to the city and tie me to fences, doorknobs.

"You slept in," he says. He begins to shift himself over onto me but I look at the sun, it's late, eight-thirty almost. In the main room I can hear metal on metal, they're up.

"There's no hurry," he says, but I push him away and get dressed.

Anna is making food, scraping a spoon in the frying pan. She has her purple tunic on and her white bellbottoms, urban costume, and her makeup is slabbed down over her face like a visor.

"I thought I'd do it," she says, "so you two could sleep in." She must have heard the door opening and closing in the night; she produces a smile, warm, conspiratorial, and I know what circuits are closing in her head: by screwing Joe she's brought us back together. Saving the world, everyone wants to; men think they can do it with guns, women with their bodies, love conquers all, conquerors love all, mirages raised by words.

She dishes out breakfast. It's baked beans from a can, the usual morning food is gone.

"Pork and beans and musical fruit, the more you eat the more you toot," David says and quacks like Daffy Duck, jaunty, mimicking satisfaction.

Anna helps him, co-operative community life; she taps him on the knuckles with her fork and says "Oh you." Then she remembers and adjusts to her Tragedy mask: "How long will it take you, in the village I mean?"

"I don't know," I say. "Not very long."

We pack and I help them carry the baggage down, my own also, caseful of alien words and failed pictures, canvas bundle of clothes, nothing I need. They sit on the dock talking; Anna is smoking, she's reduced to the last one.

"Christ," she says, "I'll be glad to hit the city. Stock up again."

I go up the steps once more to make sure they haven't left anything. The jays are there, flowing from tree to tree, voices semaphoring, tribal; they retreat to the upper branches, they still haven't decided whether I can be trusted. The cabin is the way we found it; when Evans arrives I'll snap the lock.

"You should take the canoes up before he comes," I say when I'm back down. "They go in the toolshed."

"Right," David says. He consults his watch, but they don't get up. They have the camera out, they're discussing the movie; the zipper bag of equipment is beside them, the tripod, the reels of film in their cannisters.

"I figure we can start cutting it in two or three weeks," David says, his version of a pro. "We'll take it into the lab first thing."

"There's part of a reel left," Anna says. "You should get her, you got me but you never got her." She looks at me, fumes ascending from her nose and mouth.

"Now that's an idea," David says. "The rest of us are in it, she's the only one who isn't." He assesses me. "Where would we fit her in though? We don't have anyone fucking yet; but I'd have to do it," he says to Joe, "we need you running the camera."

"I could run the camera," Anna says, "you could both do it," and everyone laughs.

They get up after a while and hoist the red canoe, one at each end, and carry it up the hill. I stay with Anna on the dock.

"Is my nose peeling?" she says, rubbing it. From her handbag she takes a round gilt compact with violets on the cover. She opens it, unclosing her other self, and runs her fingertip around the corners of her mouth, left one, right one; then she unswivels a pink stick and dots her cheeks and blends them, changing her shape, performing the only magic left to her.

Rump on a packsack, harem cushion, pink on the cheeks and black discreetly around the eyes, as red as blood as black as ebony, a seamed and folded imitation of a magazine picture that is itself an imitation of a woman who is also an imitation, the original nowhere, hairless lobed angel in the same heaven where God is a circle, captive princess in someone's head. She is locked in, she isn't allowed to eat or shit or cry or give birth, nothing goes in, nothing comes out. She takes her clothes off or puts them on, paper doll wardrobe, she copulates under strobe lights with the man's torso while his brain watches from its glassed-in control cubicle at the other end of the room, her face twists into poses of exultation and total abandonment, that is all. She is not bored, she has no other interests.

Anna sits, darkness in her eye sockets, skull with a candle. She clicks the compact shut and stubs out her cigarette against the dock; I remember the way she was crying, climbing up the sand hill, it was yesterday, since then she has crystallized. The machine is gradual, it takes a little of you at a time, it leaves the shell. It was all right as long as they stuck to dead things, the dead can defend themselves, to be half dead is worse. They did it to each other also, without knowing.

I unzip the bag with the camera equipment and lift out the cannisters of film.

"What're you doing?" Anna says, listlessly however.

I unwind the film, standing full in the sun, and let it spiral into the lake. "You better not do that," Anna says, "they'll kill you." But she doesn't interfere, she doesn't call them.

When I've unravelled the reels I open the back of the camera. The film coils onto the sand under the water, weighted down by its containers; the invisible captured images are swimming away into the lake like tadpoles, Joe and David beside their defeated log, axemen, arms folded, Anna with no clothes on jumping off the end of the dock, finger up, hundreds of tiny naked Annas no longer bottled and shelved.

I study her to see if her release has made any difference, but the green eyes regard me unaltered from the enamel face. "They'll get you," she says, doleful as a prophet. "You shouldn't have done it."

They're at the top of the hill now, coming back for the other canoe. I run quickly towards it, flip it over right side up, throw a paddle inside and drag it along the dock.

"Hey!" David calls. "What're you doing?" They're almost here, Anna watches me, biting a knuckle, she can't decide whether or not to tell: if she keeps quiet they'll treat her as an accomplice.

I slide the canoe stern first into the water, squat, step in, shove.

"She dumped out your film," Anna says behind me.

I push the blade into the water, I don't turn, I can hear them peering down into the lake.

"Shit," David says, "shit, shit, oh shit, why the shit didn't you stop her?"

When I'm as far as the sand point I look back. Anna stands, arms slack at her sides, uninvolved; David is kneeling, his hands fishing in the water, pulling up the film in spaghetti handfuls though he must know it's futile, everything has escaped.

Joe is not there. He appears then at the top of the sand cliff, running, halting. He yells my name, furiously: if he had a rock he would throw it.

The canoe glides, carrying the two of us, around past the leaning trees and out of range. It's too late for them to get the other canoe and follow; probably they haven't thought of it, surprise attacks work by confusing. The direction is clear. I see I've been planning this, for how long I can't tell.

I go along near the trees, boat and arms one movement, amphibian; the water closes behind me, no track. The land bends and we bend with it, a narrowing and then a space and I'm safe, hidden in the shore maze.

Here there are boulders; they loom under the water, brown shadows like clouds or threats, barricade. Slope of ground on either side, rock hung with creepers. The lake floor, once land floor, slants upward, so shallow now a motor could not pass. Another turning and I'm in the bay, landlocked swamp, layer of tepid water with reeds and cat-tails nosing up through the black vegetable ooze, around the sawed stumps of the once tower-high trees. This is where I threw the dead things and rinsed the tins and jars.

I float, no need to paddle. Further in, the trees they didn't cut before the flood are marooned, broken and grey-white, tipped on their sides, their giant contorted roots bleached and skinless; on the sodden trunks are colonies of plants, feeding on disintegration, laurel, sundew the insect-eater, its toenail-sized leaves sticky with red hairs. Out of the leaf nests the flowers rise, pure white, flesh of gnats and midges, petals now, metamorphosis.

I lie down on the bottom of the canoe and wait. The still water gathers the heat; birds, off in the forest a woodpecker, somewhere a thrush. Through the trees the sun glances; the swamp around me smoulders, energy of decay turning to growth, green fire. I remember the heron; by now it will be insects, frogs, fish, other herons. My body also changes, the creature in me, plant-animal, sends out filaments in me; I ferry it secure between death and life, I multiply.

The motor approaching wakes me: it's out on the lake, it will be Evans. I beach the canoe, knot the rope to a tree. They won't be expecting me, not from this direction; I have to make sure they leave with him as they should, it would be their way to pretend but stay behind to catch me when I come back.

It's less than a quarter of a mile through the trees, swerving to avoid branches, careful where I step, along the vestiges of the coded trail to where the laboratory shelves were, if I didn't know the trail was there I could never find it. As Evans' boat pulls into the dock I am behind them, near the piled wood, head down and lying flat, I can see them through the screen of plant stems.

They stoop, they're loading the things into the.boat. I wonder if they're taking mine as well, my clothes, fragments of pictures.

They stand talking with Evans, their voices low, inaudible; but they'll be explaining, they'll have to invent some reason, accident, say why I'm not with them. They will be plotting, a stategy for recapture; or will they really go off and discard me, vanish into the catacombs of the city, giving me up for lost, stashing me away in their heads with all the obsolete costumes and phrases? For them I'll soon be ancient as crew cuts and world war songs, a half-remembered face in a highschool year-book, a captured enemy medal: memorabilia, or possibly not even that.

Joe comes up the steps, shouting; Anna shouts too, shrill, like a train whistle before departure, my name. It's too late, I no longer have a name. I tried for all those years to be civil-ized but I'm not and I'm through pretending.

Joe goes around to the front of the cabin, concealed from me. After a minute he reappears, stumping back down the hill to them, shoulders sloped in defeat. Perhaps by now he understands.

They clamber into the boat. Anna pauses for a moment. turned directly towards me, face in the sunlight puzzled, oddly forlorn: does she see me, is she going to wave goodbye? Then the others reach out hands to her and lift her in, a gesture that looks from a distance almost like love.

The boat chugs backwards into the bay, then swings into forward and roars. Bullhead Evans at the wheel, checkshirted and stolid, American, they are all Americans now. But they are really going, really gone, a ringing in my ears and then a silence. I get to my feet slowly, my body is cramped from not moving; on the bare flesh of my legs are the imprints of leaves and twigs.

I walk to the hill and scan the shoreline, finding the place, opening, where they disappeared: checking, reassuring. It's true, I am by myself; this is what I wanted, to stay here alone. From any rational point of view I am absurd; but there are no longer any rational points of view.

Chapter Twenty-Two

They've locked the doors, on the toolshed, on the cabin; it was Joe, he may have assumed I'd take the canoe to the village. No, it was ill will. I shouldn't have left the keys hanging on the nail, I should have put them in my pocket. But it was stupid of them to think they could keep me out. Soon they will reach the village, the car, the city; what are they saying about me now? That I was running away; but to go with them would have been running away, the truth is here.

I stand on the front step and lean sideways, clutching the windowledge, looking in. The canvas packsack with my clothes has been moved, it's back inside now, on the table with my case; beside it is Anna's detective novel, her last one, cold comfort but comfort, death is logical, there's always a motive. Perhaps that's why she read them, for the theology.

Sun gone, sky darkening, it may rain later. Clouds building over the hills, anvils, ominous hammerheads, it will be a storm; it might miss though, sometimes they eddy for days, approaching but never striking. I'll have to get inside. Breaking into my own house, go in and out the window they used to sing, holding their arms up like bridges; as we have done before.

The handbarrow is underneath the cabin, beside the stacked wood where it was always kept, two poles with boards nailed across like rungs. I haul it out and prop it against the wall under the window, the one with no screen. The window is hooked on the inside at the corners, I'll have to break four of the little squares of glass. I do it with a rock, my head turned away, eyes closed because of the splinters. I reach carefully in through the jagged holes and undo the hooks and lift the window inwards onto the couch. If I could open the toolshed I could use the screwdriver to take the padlock hasp off the door, but the toolshed has no windows. Axe and machete inside it, saw, metal utensils.

I step on the couch and then on the floor, I'm in. I sweep up the broken glass; after that I hook the window back in place. It will be a nuisance, climbing in and out, removing the window each time, but the other windows have screens and I've nothing to cut them with. I could try the knife: if I had to leave in a hurry it would be better to use one of the back windows, they're nearer the ground.

I've succeeded; I don't know what to do now. I pause in the middle of the room, listening: no wind, stillness, held breath of the lake, the trees.

To be busy I unpack my clothes again and hang them on the nails in my room. My mother's jacket is back, I last saw it in Anna's room, it's been shifted. My footsteps are the only sounds, reverberation of shoes on wood.

There must be something that comes next but the power has drained away, my fingers are empty as gloves, eyes ordinary, nothing guides me.

I sit down at the table and leaf through an old magazine, shepherds knitting their own socks, weather gnarling their faces, women in laced bodices and red lipstick balancing washing baskets on their heads, smiling to show their teeth and happiness; rubber plantations and deserted temples, jungle crawling over the serene carved gods. Ring from a wet cup on the cover, printed there yesterday or ten years ago.

I open a can of peaches and eat two of the yellow fibrous halves, sugary juice dribbling from the spoon. Then I lie down

on the couch and sleep descends over my face, black oblong,
dreamless.

When I wake up the diffused light outside is further west, it
feels late, it must be almost six, dinner hour; David had the
only watch. Hunger is there in me, a contained whimper. I
unhook the window and climb out, one foot on the wobbling
handbarrow, scraping my knee as I let myself drop to the
ground. I should build a ladder; but there are no implements,
no boards.

I go down to the garden. I've forgotten the knife and the
bowl but they aren't needed, fingers will do. I unlatch the gate,
the chicken wire walls are around me; outside the fence the
trees droop as though wilting, the plants inside are pale in
the greyish light; the air is heavy, oppressive. I start to pull
up the onions and the carrots.

I'm crying finally, it's the first time, I watch myself doing
it: I'm crouching down beside the lettuces, flowers finished
now, gone to seed, my breath knots, my body tightens against
it; the water fills my mouth, fish taste. But I'm not mourning,
I'm accusing them, *Why did you?* They chose it, they had
control over their death, they decided it was time to leave and
they left, they set up this barrier. They didn't consider how
I would feel, who would take care of me. I'm furious because
they let it happen.

"Here I am," I call. "I'm here!" Voice rising and rising
with the frustration and then the terror of hearing no answer,
the time we were playing after supper and I hid too well, too
far away and they couldn't find me. The treetrunks are so
much alike, the same size, the same colour, impossible to
retrace the path, instead locate the sun, the direction, which-
ever way you go you're bound to hit water. The dangerous
thing is to panic, to walk in circles.

"I'm here!" But nothing happens. I wipe the salt off my
face, my fingers earth-smeared.

If I will it, if I pray, I can bring them back. They're here now, I can sense them waiting, beyond sight on the path or in the long grass outside the fence, they are pulling against me but I can make them come out, from wherever it is they are hiding.

I start a fire in the stove and cook the food in the darkening room. There's no reason to set out plates; I eat from the pot and the frying pan with a spoon. I'll save the dirty dishes till there are enough; when the dishwasher pail is full I will have to lower it through the window with a rope.

I climb out again and set the scraps from the tinned meat on the tray for the birds. Deep grey, the clouds descending, closing in; the puffs of wind have begun, they advance across the lake like shudders; to the south there's a column of rain. Flickers of light but no thunder, gust of leaves.

I walk up the hill to the outhouse, forcing myself to go slowly, holding the panic at a distance, looking at it. Inside I hook the door shut, it's doors I'm afraid of because I can't see through them, it's the door opening by itself in the wind I'm afraid of. I run back down the path, telling myself to stop it, I'm old enough, I'm old.

The power would have protected me but it's gone, exhausted, no more use now than silver bullets or the sign of the cross. But the house will defend me, it's the right shape. Back inside I put the window up again, hooking it to the frame, barricading myself in, wood bars. The four broken panes, how can I close them. I try stuffing them with pages torn from the magazines and crumpled, *National Geographic, Macleans,* but it doesn't work, the holes are too big, the wads of paper fall to the floor. If only I had nails, a hammer.

I light the lamp but the air drafting in through the broken window makes it flutter and turn blue, and with the lamp on I can't see what's happening outside. I blow it out and sit in darkness, listening to the gush of the wind, but it doesn't rain.

After a while I decide to go to bed. I'm not tired, I slept in the afternoon, but there's nothing else to do. In my room

I stand for a long time wondering why I'm afraid to take off my clothes: am I worried that they'll come back for me, if they do I'll have to get out quickly; but they wouldn't try it in a storm, Evans knows better than that, the open lake is the worst place because of the electricity, flesh and water both conduct.

I tie back the curtain so there will be more light. My mother's jacket is hanging on a nail beside the window, there's nobody in it; I press my forehead against it. Leather smell, the smell of loss; irrecoverable. But I can't think about that. I lie down on the bed in my clothes and in a moment the first rain hits the roof. It patters, changes to a steady drumming, sound of an avalanche, surrounding. I feel the lake rising, up over the shore and the hill, the trees toppling into it like sand collapsing, roots overturned, the house unmoored and floating like a boat, rocking and rocking.

In the middle of the night silence wakes me, the rain has stopped. Blank dark, I can see nothing, I try to move my hands but I can't. The fear arrives like waves, like footfalls, it has no center; it encloses me like armour, it's my skin that is afraid, rigid. They want to get in, they want me to open the windows, the door, they can't do it by themselves. I'm the only one, they are depending on me but I don't know any longer who they are; however they come back they won't be the same, they will have changed. I willed it, I called to them, that they should arrive is logical; but logic is a wall, I built it, on the other side is terror.

Above on the roof is the finger-tapping of water dripping from the trees. I hear breathing, withheld, observant, not in the house but all around it.

Chapter Twenty-Three

In the morning I remember the window outline, beginning to emerge; I must have been watching till nearly dawn. Then I think it might have been a dream, the kind that creates the illusion of being awake.

For breakfast I eat canned stew, heating it first in a pot, and instant coffee. There are too many windows, I move so I'm sitting on the wall bench, from there I can see all of them.

I stack the dishes in the pan with the ones from last night and pour the rest of the hot water over them. Then I turn to the mirror to brush my hair.

But when I pick up the brush there is a surge of fear in my hand, the power is there again in a different form, it must have seeped up through the ground during the lightning. I know that the brush is forbidden, I must stop being in the mirror. I look for the last time at my distorted glass face: eyes lightblue in dark red skin, hair standing tangled out from my head, reflection intruding between my eyes and vision. Not to see myself but to see. I reverse the mirror so it's toward the wall, it no longer traps me, Anna's soul closed in the gold compact, that and not the camera is what I should have broken.

I unfasten the window and go out; at once the fear leaves me like a hand lifting from my throat. There must be rules: places I'm permitted to be, other places I'm not. I'll have to listen carefully, if I trust them they will tell me what is allowed. I ought to have let them in, it may have been the only chance they will give me.

The enclosure with the swing and the sandpile is forbidden, I know that without touching it. I walk down to the lake. It is flat calm, the water is pollen-streaked, mist is drifting up off the bays and from behind the islands, the sun burning it away as it rises, the sun itself hot and bright as light through a lens. Something glimmers out on the surface, a swimming animal or a dead log; when there is no wind things venture out from the shore. The air smells of earth, midsummer.

I step on the dock: the fear says No, I can be near the lake but not on the dock. I wash my hands from the flat stone. If I do everything in the right order, if I think of nothing else. What sacrifice, what do they want?

When I'm certain I've guessed what is required I go back to the cabin, enter it. The fire I made for breakfast is still smouldering: I add another stick of wood and open the draft.

I snap the catches on my case and take out the drawings and the typescript, *Quebec Folk Tales,* it's easily replaceable for them in the city, and my bungled princesses, the Golden Phoenix awkward and dead as a mummified parrot. The pages bunch in my hands; I add them one by one so the fire will not be smothered, then the paint tubes and brushes, this is no longer my future. There must be some way of cancelling the samsonite case, it can't be burned. I draw the big knife across it, x-ing it out.

I slip the ring from my left hand, non-husband, he is the next thing I must discard finally, and drop it into the fire, altar, it may not melt but it will at least be purified, the blood will burn off. Everything from history must be eliminated, the circles and the arrogant square pages. I rummage under the mattress and bring out the scrapbooks, ripping them up, the ladies, dress forms with decorated china heads, the suns and the moons, the rabbits and their archaic eggs, my false peace, his wars, aeroplanes and tanks and the helmeted explorers;

perhaps at the other side of the world my brother feels the weight lifting, freedom feathering his arms. Even the guides, the miraculous double woman and the god with horns, they must be translated. The ladies on the wall too with their watermelon breasts and lampshade skirts, all my artifacts.

Theirs too, the map torn from the wall, the rock paintings, left to me by my father's will; and the album, the sequence of my mother's life, the confining photographs. My own faces curl, blacken, the imitation mother and father change to flat ashes. It is time that separates us, I was a coward, I would not let them into my age, my place. Now I must enter theirs.

When the paper things are burned I smash the glasses and plates and the chimney of the lamp. I rip one page from each of the books, Boswell and *The Mystery at Sturbridge,* the Bible and the common mushrooms and *Log Cabin Construction,* to burn through all the words would take too long. Everything I can't break, frying pan, enamel bowl, spoons and forks, I throw on the floor. After that I use the big knife to slash once through the blankets, the sheets and the beds and the tents and at the end my own clothes and my mother's grey leather jacket, my father's grey felt hat, the raincoats: these husks are not needed any longer, I abolish them, I have to clear a space.

When nothing is left intact and the fire is only smouldering I leave, carrying one of the wounded blankets with me, I will need it until the fur grows. The house shuts with a click behind me.

I untie my feet from the shoes and walk down to the shore; the earth is damp, cold, pockmarked with raindrops. I pile the blanket on the rock and step into the water and lie down. When every part of me is wet I take off my clothes, peeling them away from my flesh like wallpaper. They sway beside me, inflated, the sleeves bladders of air.

My back is on the sand, my head rests against the rock, innocent as plankton; my hair spreads out, moving and fluid in the water. The earth rotates, holding my body down to it as it holds the moon; the sun pounds in the sky, red flames and rays pulsing from it, searing away the wrong form that encases me, dry rain soaking through me, warming the blood egg I carry. I dip my head beneath the water, washing my eyes.

Inshore a loon; it lowers its head, then lifts it again and calls. It sees me but it ignores me, accepts me as part of the land.

When I am clean I come up out of the lake, leaving my false body floated on the surface, a cloth decoy; it jiggles in the waves I make, nudges gently against the dock.

They offered clothing as a token, formerly; that was partial but the gods are demanding, absolute, they want all.

The sun is three-quarters, I have become hungry. The food in the cabin is forbidden, I'm not allowed to go back into that cage, wooden rectangle. Also tin cans and jars are forbidden; they are glass and metal. I head for the garden and prowl through it, then squat, wrapped in my blanket. I eat the green peas out of their shells and the raw yellow beans, I scrape the carrots from the earth with my fingers, I will wash them in the lake first. There is one late strawberry, I find it among the matted weeds and suckers. Red foods, heart colour, they are the best kind, they are sacred; then yellow, then blue; green foods are mixed from blue and yellow. I pull up one of the beets and scratch the dirt from it and gnaw at it but the rind is tough, I'm not strong enough yet.

At sunset I devour the washed carrots, taking them from the grass where I've concealed them, and part of a cabbage. The outhouse is forbidden so I leave my dung, droppings, on the ground and kick earth over. All animals with dens do that.

I hollow a lair near the woodpile, dry leaves underneath and dead branches leaned over, with fresh needle branches woven to cover. Inside it I curl with the blanket over my head. There are mosquitoes, they bite through; it's best not to slap them, the blood smell brings others. I sleep in relays like a cat, my stomach hurts. Around me the space rustles; owl sound, across the lake or inside me, distance contracts. A light wind, the small waves talking against the shore, multilingual water.

Chapter Twenty-Four

The light wakes me, speckled through the roof branches. My bones ache, hunger is loose in me, belly a balloon, floating shark stomach. It's hot, the sun is almost at noon, I've slept most of the morning. I crawl outside and run towards the garden where the food is.

The gate stops me. Yesterday I could go in but not today: they are doing it gradually. I lean against the fence, my feet pawprinting the mud damp from the rain, the dew, the lake oozing up through the ground. Then my belly cramps and I step to one side and lie down in the long grass. A frog is there, leopard frog with green spots and gold-rimmed eyes, ancestor. It includes me, it shines, nothing moves but its throat breathing.

I rest on the ground, head propped on hands, trying to forget the hunger, looking through the wire hexagons at the garden: rows, squares, stakes, markers. The plants are flourishing, they grow almost visibly, sucking moisture up through the roots and succulent stems, their leaves sweating, flushed in the sunrays to a violent green, weeds and legitimate plants alike, there is no difference. Under the ground the worms twine, pink veins.

The fence is impregnable; it can keep out everything but weed seeds, birds, insects and the weather. Beneath it is a two-foot-deep moat, paved with broken glass, smashed jars and bottles, and covered with gravel and earth, the wood-chucks and skunks can't burrow under. Frogs and snakes get through but they are permitted.

The garden is a stunt, a trick. It could not exist without the fence.

Now I understand the rule. They can't be anywhere that's marked out, enclosed: even if I opened the doors and fences they could not pass in, to houses and cages, they can move only in the spaces between them, they are against borders. To talk with them I must approach the condition they themselves have entered; in spite of my hunger I must resist the fence, I'm too close now to turn back.

But there must be something else I can eat, something that is not forbidden. I think of what I might catch, crayfish, leeches, no not yet. Along the trail the edible plants, the mushrooms, I know the poisonous kinds and the ones we used to collect, some of them can be eaten raw.

There are raspberries on the canes, shrivelled and not many but they are red. I suck those, their sweetness, sourness, piercing in my mouth, teeth crackling on the seeds. Into the trail, tunnel, cool of the trees, as I walk I search the ground for shapes I can eat, anything. Provisions, they will provide, they have always favoured survival.

I find the six-leaved plants again, two of them, and dig up the crisp white roots and chew them, not waiting to take them back to the lake to wash them. Earth caked beneath my jagged nails.

The mushrooms are still there, the deadly white one, I'll save that till I'm immune, ready, and the yellow food, yellow fingers. By now many of them are too old, wrinkled, but I break off the softer ones. I hold them in my mouth a long time before swallowing, they taste musty, mildewed canvas, I'm not sure of them.

What else, what else? Enough for a while. I sit down, wrapping myself in the blanket which is damp from the grass, my feet have gone cold. I will need other things, perhaps I can catch a bird or a fish, with my hands, that will be fair. Inside me it is growing, they take what they require, if I don't feed it it will absorb my teeth, bones, my hair will thin, come out in handfuls. But I put it there, I invoked it, the fur god with tail and horns, already forming. The mothers of gods, how do they feel, voices and light glaring from the belly, do they feel sick, dizzy? Pain squeezes my stomach, I bend, head pressed against knees.

Slowly I retrace the trail. Something has happened to my eyes, my feet are released, they alternate, several inches from the ground. I'm ice-clear, transparent, my bones and the child inside me showing through the green webs of my flesh, the ribs are shadows, the muscles jelly, the trees are like this too, they shimmer, their cores glow through the wood and bark.

The forest leaps upward, enormous, the way it was before they cut it, columns of sunlight frozen; the boulders float, melt, everything is made of water, even the rocks. In one of the languages there are no nouns, only verbs held for a longer moment.

The animals have no need for speech, why talk when you are a word

I lean against a tree, I am a tree leaning

I break out again into the bright sun and crumple, head against the ground

I am not an animal or a tree, I am the thing in which the trees and animals move and grow, I am a place

I have to get up, I get up. Through the ground, break surface, I'm standing now; separate again. I pull the blanket over my shoulders, head forward.

I can hear the jays, crying and crying as if they've found an enemy or food. They are near the cabin, I walk towards them up the hill. I see them in the trees and swooping between the trees, the air forming itself into birds, they continue to call.

Then I see her. She is standing in front of the cabin, her hand stretched out, she is wearing her grey leather jacket; her hair is long, down to her shoulders in the style of thirty years ago, before I was born; she is turned half away from me, I can see only the side of her face. She doesn't move, she is feeding them: one perches on her wrist, another on her shoulder.

I've stopped walking. At first I feel nothing except a lack of surprise: that is where she would be, she has been standing there all along. Then as I watch and it doesn't change I'm afraid, I'm cold with fear, I'm afraid it isn't real, paper doll cut by my eyes, burnt picture, if I blink she will vanish.

She must have sensed it, my fear. She turns her head quietly and looks at me, past me, as though she knows something is there but she can't quite see it. The jays cry again, they fly up from her, the shadows of their wings ripple over the ground and she's gone.

I go up to where she was. The jays are there in the trees, cawing at me; there are a few scraps on the feeding tray still, they've knocked some to the ground. I squint up at them, trying to see her, trying to see which one she is; they hop, twitch their feathers, turn their heads, fixing me first with one eye, then the other.

Chapter Twenty-Five

It's day again, my body jumps out of sleep. What I heard was a powerboat, attacking. It's almost too late, they were pulling around into the bay and slowing and nearly to the dock when I woke up. I scramble on hands and knees out of my den, blanket over me, brown plaid camouflage, and run stooping further back among the trees and flatten, worming into a thicket, hazel bushes, where I can see.

They may have been sent to hunt for me, perhaps the others asked them to, they may be the police; or they may be sightseers, curious tourists. Evans will have told at the store, the whole village will know. Or the war may have started, the invasion, they are Americans.

They can't be trusted. They'll mistake me for a human being, a naked woman wrapped in a blanket: possibly that's what they've come here for, if it's running around loose, ownerless, why not take it. They won't be able to tell what I really am. But if they guess my true form, identity, they will shoot me or bludgeon in my skull and hang me up by the feet from a tree.

They're hulking out of the boat now, four or five of them. I can't see them clearly, their faces, the stems and leaves are in the way; but I can smell them and the scent bring nausea, it's stale air, bus stations and nicotine smoke, mouths lined with soiled plush, acid taste of copper wiring or money. Their skins are red, green in squares, blue in lines, and it's a minute before I remember that these are fake skins, flags. Their real skins above the collars are white and plucked, with tufts of hair on top, piebald blend of fur and no fur like mouldy sausages or the rumps of baboons. They are evolving, they are halfway to machine, the leftover flesh atrophied and diseased, porous like an appendix.

Two of them climb the hill to the cabin. They are talking, their voices are distinct but they penetrate my ears as sounds only, foreign radio. It must be either English or French but I can't recognize it as any language I've ever heard or known. Scrapes and grunts, they're getting in, through the door or the open window, crunch of their boots inside on the broken glass. One of them laughs, spike scratched on slate.

The other three are still on the dock. Then they shout: they must have found my clothes, one is kneeling down. Is it Joe, I try to picture what Joe looks like. But it makes no difference, he wouldn't help me, he would be on their side; he may have given them the keys.

The two come out of the cabin and thud down to the dock again, their false skins flapping. They cluster, they chitter and sizzle like a speeded-up tape, the forks and spoons on the ends of their arms waving excitedly. Perhaps they think I drowned myself, that would be the kind of blunder they would make.

Keep quiet I say, I bite into my arm but I can't hold it back, the laughter extrudes. It startles me, I stop at once but it's too late, they've heard me. Rubber feet stomping off the dock and bulletproof heads moving towards me, who could they be, David and Joe, Claude from the village, Evans, Malmstrom the spy, the Americans, the humans, they're here because I wouldn't sell. I don't own it, nobody owns it I tell them, you don't have to kill me. Rabbit's choices: freeze, take the chance they won't see you; then bolt.

I have a good start on them and no shoes. I run silently,

dodging branches, heading for the path to the swamp, the canoe is there, I can easily reach it first. On the open lake they could cut me off with the motorboat but if I go into the swamp, among the dead tree roots, I'll be safe, they'd have to wade for me, the mud is soft, they'll sink like bulldozers. Behind me they crash, their boots crash, language ululating, electronic signals thrown back and forth between them, hooo, hooo, they talk in numbers, the voice of reason. They clank, heavy with weapons and iron plating.

But they've half-circled and are closing, five metal fingers converging to a fist. I double back. Other tricks: up a tree, but no time and no tree is big enough. Crouch behind boulders, at night yes but not now and there are no boulders, they've pulled themselves back into the earth just when I need them. Flight, there's no alternative, though I'm praying the power has deserted me, nothing is on my side, not even the sun.

I swerve toward the lake, there's a high bank here, steep slope, sand mostly. I go over the edge and slide down it, on a knee and elbow it seems, gouging furrows, I hope they won't see the tracks. I keep the blanket over me so the white won't show and crouch with my face against the treeroots that dangle over the eroded side. Twisted: cedars. One of my feet is gashed and the arm, I can feel the blood swelling out like sap.

The clangs and shouts thrash past me and continue, further away, then nearer. I stay unmoving, don't give yourself away. Back in the woods they group: talking, laughter. Maybe they've brought food, in hampers and thermos bottles, maybe they thought of it as a picnic. My heart clenches, unclenches, I listen to it.

The sound of the starting motor prods me. I pull myself up onto the bank and squat behind the hedge of trunks, if I stay by the shore they might see me. The noise surges out from behind the point and they rocket past, so near I could hit them with a stone. I count them, making sure, five.

That is the way they are, they will not let you have peace,

they don't want you to have anything they don't have themselves. I stay on the bank, resting, licking the scratches; no fur
yet on my skin, it's too early.

I make my way back towards the cabin, resenting the gods
although perhaps they saved me, limping, blood is still
coming out of my foot but not as much. I wonder if they have
set traps; I will have to avoid my shelter. Caught animals
gnaw off their arms and legs to get free, could I do that.

I haven't had time to be hungry and even now the hunger
is detached from me, it does not insist; I must be getting used
to it, soon I will be able to go without food altogether. Later
I will search along the other trail; at the end of it is the stone
point, it has blueberry bushes.

As I approach the toolshed the fear, the power is there, in
the soles of my feet, coming out of the ground, a soundless
humming. I am forbidden to walk on the paths. Anything that
metal has touched, scarred; axe and machete cleared the trails,
order is made with knives. His job was wrong, he was really
a surveyor, he learned the trees, naming and counting them
so the others could level and excavate. He must know that by
now. I step to one side, skirting the worn places where shoes
have been, descending towards the lake.

He is standing near the fence with his back to me, looking in
at the garden. The late afternoon sunlight falls obliquely
between the treetrunks on the hill, down on him, clouding
him in an orange haze, he wavers as if through water.

He has realized he was an intruder; the cabin, the fences,
the fires and paths were violations; now his own fence excludes him, as logic excludes love. He wants it ended, the
borders abolished, he wants the forest to flow back into the
places his mind cleared: reparation.

I say Father.

He turns towards me and it's not my father. It is what my

father saw, the thing you meet when you've stayed here too long alone.

I'm not frightened, it's too dangerous for me to be frightened of it; it gazes at me for a time with its yellow eyes, wolf's eyes, depthless but lambent as the eyes of animals seen at night in the car headlights. Reflectors. It does not approve of me or disapprove of me, it tells me it has nothing to tell me, only the fact of itself.

Then its head swings away with an awkward, almost crippled motion: I do not interest it, I am part of the landscape, I could be anything, a tree, a deer skeleton, a rock.

I see now that although it isn't my father it is what my father has become. I knew he wasn't dead.

From the lake a fish jumps
An idea of a fish jumps

A fish jumps, carved wooden fish with dots painted on the sides, no, antlered fish thing drawn in red on cliffstone, protecting spirit. It hangs in the air suspended, flesh turned to icon, he has changed again, returned to the water. How many shapes can he take.

I watch it for an hour or so; then it drops and softens, the circles widen, it becomes an ordinary fish again.

When I go to the fence the footprints are there, side by side in the mud. My breath quickens, it was true, I saw it. But the prints are too small, they have toes; I place my feet in them and find that they are my own.

Chapter Twenty-Six

In the evening I make a different lair, further back and better hidden. I eat nothing but I lie down on the rocks and drink from the lake. During the night I have a dream about them, the way they were when they were alive and becoming older; they are in a boat, the green canoe, heading out of the bay.

When I wake in the morning I know they have gone finally, back into the earth, the air, the water, wherever they were when I summoned them. The rules are over. I can go anywhere now, into the cabin, into the garden, I can walk on the paths. I am the only one left alive on the island.

They were here though, I trust that. I saw them and they spoke to me, in the other language.

I'm not hungry any more but I trudge back to the cabin and climb through the window again and open a tin of yellow beans. To prefer life, I owe them that. I sit crosslegged on the wall bench and eat the beans out of the can with my fingers, a few at a time, too much at first is bad. Junk on the floor, things broken, did I do that?

David and Anna were here, they slept in the far bedroom; I remember them, but indistinctly and with nostalgia, as I remember people I once knew. They live in the city now, in a different time. I can remember him, fake husband, more clearly though, and now I feel nothing for him but sorrow.

He was neither of the things I believed, he was only a normal man, middle-aged, second-rate, selfish and kind in the average proportions; but I was not prepared for the average, its needless cruelties and lies. My brother saw the danger early. To immerse oneself, join in the war, or to be destroyed. Though there ought to be other choices.

Soon it will be autumn, then winter; the leaves will turn by late August, as early as October it will begin to snow and it will keep on until the snow is level with the tops of the windows or the bottom of the roof, the lake will freeze solid. Or before that they'll close the floodgates on the dam and the water will rise, I'll watch it day by day, perhaps that's why they came in the motorboat, not to hunt but to warn me. In any case I can't stay here forever, there isn't enough food. The garden won't last and the tins and bottles will give out; the link between me and the factories is broken, I have no money.

If they were searchers they will go back and say maybe that they saw me, maybe that they only thought they did. If they weren't searchers they'll say nothing.

I could take the canoe that's roped up in the swamp and paddle the ten miles to the village, now, tomorrow, when I've eaten and I'm strong enough. Then back to the city and the pervasive menace, the Americans. They exist, they're advancing, they must be dealt with, but possibly they can be watched and predicted and stopped without being copied.

No gods to help me now, they're questionable once more, theoretical as Jesus. They've receded, back to the past, inside the skull, is it the same place. They'll never appear to me again, I can't afford it; from now on I'll have to live in the usual way, defining them by their absence; and love by its failures, power by its loss, its renunciation. I regret them; but they give only one kind of truth, one hand.

No total salvation, resurrection, Our father, Our mother, I pray, Reach down for me, but it won't work: they dwindle, grow, become what they were, human. Something I never gave them credit for; but their totalitarian innocence was my own.

I try to think for the first time what it was like to be them: our father, islanding his life, protecting both us and himself, in the midst of war and in a poor country, the effort it must have taken to sustain his illusions of reason and benevolent order, and perhaps he didn't. Our mother, collecting the seasons and the weather and her children's faces, the meticulous records that allowed her to omit the other things, the pain and isolation and whatever it was she was fighting against, something in a vanished history, I can never know. They are out of reach now, they belong to themselves, more than ever.

I set the half-empty tin down on the table and walk carefully across the floor, my bare feet avoiding the broken glass. I turn the mirror around: in it there's a creature neither animal nor human, furless, only a dirty blanket, shoulders huddled over into a crouch, eyes staring blue as ice from the deep sockets; the lips move by themselves. This was the stereotype, straws in the hair, talking nonsense or not talking at all. To have someone to speak to and words that can be understood: their definition of sanity.

That is the real danger now, the hospital or the zoo, where we are put, species and individual, when we can no longer cope. They would never believe it's only a natural woman, state of nature, they think of that as a tanned body on a beach with washed hair waving like scarves; not this, face dirt-caked and streaked, skin grimed and scabby, hair like a frayed bathmat stuck with leaves and twigs. A new kind of centrefold.

I laugh, and a noise comes out like something being killed: a mouse, a bird?

Chapter Twenty-Seven

This above all, to refuse to be a victim. Unless I can do that I can do nothing. I have to recant, give up the old belief that I am powerless and because of it nothing I can do will ever hurt anyone. A lie which was always more disastrous than the truth would have been. The word games, the winning and losing games are finished; at the moment there are no others but they will have to be invented, withdrawing is no longer possible and the alternative is death.

I drop the blanket on the floor and go into my dismantled. room. My spare clothes are here, knife slashes in them but I can still wear them. I dress, clumsily, unfamiliar with buttons; I re-enter my own time.

But I bring with me from the distant past five nights ago the time-traveller, the primaeval one who will have to learn, shape of a goldfish now in my belly, undergoing its watery changes. Word furrows potential already in its proto-brain, untravelled paths. No god and perhaps not real, even that is uncertain; I can't know yet, it's too early. But I assume it: if I die it dies, if I starve it starves with me. It might be the first one, the first true human; it must be born, allowed.

I'm outside in the garden when the boat comes. It isn't Evans; it's Paul's boat, thick and slow and painted white, he built it himself. Paul is at the back, beside the antique motor; in the front is Joe.

I go out through the gate and retreat behind the trees, white birches clumped beside the path, not hurrying, not running away but cautious.

The motor cuts, the nose of the boat bumps the dock. Paul stands up with an oar, pulling in; Joe gets out and ropes the boat and takes several steps towards the land.

He calls my name, then pauses, "Are you here?" Echo: here, here?

He must have been waiting in the village, the searchers must have told him they'd seen me, perhaps he was with them. He stayed behind when David and Anna went away in their car, or he drove to the city with them and then hitched back, walked back, what's important is that he's here, a mediator, an ambassador, offering me something: captivity in any of its forms, a new freedom?

I watch him, my love for him useless as a third eye or a possibility. If I go with him we will have to talk, wooden houses are obsolete, we can no longer live in spurious peace by avoiding each other, the way it was before, we will have to begin. For us it's necessary, the intercession of words; and we will probably fail, sooner or later, more or less painfully. That's normal, it's the way it happens now and I don't know whether it's worth it or even if I can depend on him, he may have been sent as a trick. But he isn't an American, I can see that now; he isn't anything, he is only half-formed, and for that reason I can trust him.

To trust is to let go. I tense forward, towards the demands and questions, though my feet do not move yet.

He calls for me again, balancing on the dock which is neither land nor water, hands on hips, head thrown back and eyes scanning. His voice is annoyed: he won't wait much longer. But right now he waits.

The lake is quiet, the trees surround me, asking and giving nothing.

Now you can order superb titles directly from Virago

☐ Alias Grace	Margaret Atwood	£6.99
☐ Bluebeard's Egg and Other Stories	Margaret Atwood	£6.99
☐ Bones and Murder	Margaret Atwood	£6.99
☐ Cat's Eye	Margaret Atwood	£6.99
☐ The Edible Woman	Margaret Atwood	£6.99
☐ Good Bones	Margaret Atwood	£6.99
☐ Lady Oracle	Margaret Atwood	£6.99
☐ Murder in the Dark	Margaret Atwood	£6.99
☐ The Robber Bride	Margaret Atwood	£6.99

Please allow for postage and packing: **Free UK delivery.**
Europe; add 25% of retail price; Rest of World; 45% of retail price.

To order any of the above or any other Virago titles, please call our credit card orderline or fill in this coupon and send/fax it to:

Virago, 250 Western Avenue, London, W3 6XZ, UK.
Fax 0181 324 5678   Telephone 0181 324 5516

☐ I enclose a UK bank cheque made payable to Virago for £ ....

☐ Please charge £.............. to my Access, Visa, Delta, Switch Card No.

☐☐☐☐☐☐☐☐☐☐☐☐☐☐☐☐☐☐☐

Expiry Date ☐☐☐☐   Switch Issue No. ☐☐

NAME (Block letters please) ....

ADDRESS ....

....

....

Postcode ....Telephone ....

Signature ....

Please allow 28 days for delivery within the UK. Offer subject to price and availability.

Please do not send any further mailings from companies carefully selected by Virago ☐